I0788793

The Gathering Place

by
Elizabeth Ferrell Casey

Crippled Beagle Publishing
Knoxville, Tennessee, USA
www.crippledbeaglepublishing.com

Cover design: Maria Loysa-Bel Nueve-de los Angeles

Paperback ISBN 978-1-965334-25-6
Hardcover ISBN 978-1-965334-26-3

Library of Congress Control Number: 2024927088

Printed in the United States of America

To the Mrs. McCrackens.

And to my home team
Mark, Sarah, Caroline.

Some journeys take us far from home. Some adventures lead us to our destiny.
~ C.S. Lewis

It was recently discovered our ancestors may have been writing stories about the supernatural as long as a half a million years ago. Etchings of beings, half-human and half-animal, found on limestone cave walls on the island of Sulawesi in Indonesia. They are called therianthropes, and they can also be found in Egyptian, Hindu, Christian, African, and American Indian writings and art. Therianthropes can represent good or evil, demon or deity, but they all have one thing in common: the attempt at telling a story. A God story.

Most of us have God stories. Stories that come from our religions. Our cultures. Our people. Our tribes. Some adopt their story with no need for examination. Some toss their story. Some evaluate their story and integrate parts of it into their lives in a way that makes sense to them.

And then, well, there are the seekers.

The seekers do deep dives into their stories. We search out the challenging books. We lean into the uncomfortable conversations. We research. We obsess. We ruminate. It's in our DNA. It's in our blood. And when we feel like we have something worth sharing, we write books. We draw therianthropes on walls of caves.

My God story began in my small Southern town where I learned my first life lessons and found my first teachers—as most of us do. And, well, I was not the easiest of students—as seekers often aren't. A "spirited child," my Gram used to say. My dad used to add, "with a wicked mean streak." I can't argue with that.

My name is Laine.

I'll start by telling you about Will. Looking back, he was a catalyst in my own God story.

Will. My pond frog. And my almost forever. Before I stumbled into my destiny.

Chapter 1

Membership

I guess Will first took notice of me in Driver's Ed class around the middle of the fall semester of our junior year. I knew that he liked me because instead of going to the gym to shoot basketball when it wasn't our day to drive, he started hanging out in the library. He would pretend to read large books while I studied or helped shelve the returns. The feeling became mutual when we ran track together that spring. Then, we became a full-fledged couple after a youth mission trip to Maryland that summer.

It never occurred to me that a guy like Will would have any real interest in me. I preferred books over most people. Will had tons of friends. He was a "prized egg." His genes were stacked with generous amounts of athleticism and brains. I think he still holds a track record at our high school. He made a thirty-one on his first try on the ACT. Honestly, he could have dated any girl in our class. And Will comes from old money. His family owns an accounting firm that is as old as our town itself.

The accounting firm, I should say. Really, it's the only one in our small, sedate town; the once stately but tired office is still nestled right there on North Main across from the courthouse. And not only does Will come from old money, he comes from a long line of deacons in our church. Basically, our church royalty. Their pictures, dating back nearly a hundred years, still on the wall across from the choir room.

And as you could probably imagine, the Marley men have a long line of pleasant, doting wives who have perfected the potatoes *au gratin* and have spent their days finding just the right shade of blue tie for their "hubby" while making sure the children are well-dressed, well-schooled, and, most importantly, don't humiliate the family in any way. And in Will's family, not one had defected to date. Of course, if there had been a defector, who would have ever known? The Marleys were professionals at public relations.

But to be William Marley's lawfully wedded wife—who could want anything more? These kinds of families, not unlike royalty, date to marry. It's a strategic business transaction. A carefully calculated chess move. For my dad, if I could marry a Marley, I basically held the winning ticket to the lottery of life. I was working my tail off to maintain my GPA and improve my ACT score to ensure my entry into Grandpa Anderson's alma mater. Of course, my dad was proud. This would be a dream come true. But that was still secondary to the possible achievement of landing a "blue blood," which was what he called people who didn't have to work like "rented mules" and pray to make ends meet like the Andersons always had.

But I wasn't "that girl." Hardly.

A dad can dream. William and Elaine Marley. Glory be. If all went as expected, we would graduate at the top of our classes. We would do mission work on our summer breaks—out of the country most likely. Never mind the people who were homeless four blocks over. I asked about that one time. Something about "the Great Commission." The people in Timbuktu needed to know about Jesus more than the guy sleeping behind the doughnut shop needed a warm bed and a meal. I remember thinking as we drove by his "camp" on the way to church, *I guess we checked him off a long time ago. He already knows about Jesus. Nobody's getting any more points in heaven for that one.*

Once I asked our youth minister, Brad, "If someone has never been told about Jesus, will they still go to hell?"

He said, rather smugly, "No. God will have mercy. They can't reject something they don't know anything about, Laine."

I, returning his smugness, replied, "Well, why tell them then? If they don't know, they have a one hundred percent chance of getting to heaven. If we tell them, it's fifty-fifty at best."

If he could have choked me, he would have. Brad grew to hate me. Looking back, I don't blame him.

Anyway. Will.

Let's see. We would most likely have a mid-June wedding following our May graduation from our respectable colleges. Honeymoon at his family's home on Sullivan Island. Or maybe be gifted a trip to somewhere exotic. A place impossible to pronounce. But we certainly would attend our home church after we returned. There was no question about that. Sunday mornings and Wednesday nights. Easter cantatas and Christmas pageants. He would go on to be senior partner of the firm. My dad could gloat endlessly. And I would spawn young, perfect Marleys that our fathers would celebrate together with fine cigars. Not to mention the flow of good content for my mother's social media. My education would not be wasted, of course. A woman should be properly educated as long she used that education, as Will's mother had, on the upbringing of new bright-eyed members of "the club."

Now, there were elements of that life that I didn't really mind. And Will was actually an okay guy. Will wasn't all wrapped up in appearances. He had nothing to prove to anyone. That had been done generations before him. In the beginning, he was silly and fun-loving. He had messy auburn hair and kind, dark-chocolate brown eyes that I wanted to just crawl into some days. He had a spray of freckles across his nose that would come out in the sun. Will was the best hugger. We had our own language and volumes of inside jokes. We both loved running, anything outdoors. When we first fell in love, we talked about traveling to every single national park and sleeping under the stars. "Laine's stars," he would call them. I had always been entranced by the night sky. He seemed to barely take notice but wanted to give me every square inch of it ... in the beginning, at least. I knew if I could just conform and we did marry one day, I would be safely kept by him and the Marley name. The bills would always be paid. Our children would never want.

I know what you are thinking, and you aren't wrong. Will was more than okay. For someone.

I rarely saw Will's father, but I grew to adore Will's mom. She liked me too. She was smart and witty when you got to know her. And she contributed more to the betterment of our society in a real and genuine way than most people I know. Her charity was never on display. She preferred it that way. Truly, most people never had a clue about the depth of her selflessness. She didn't follow a lot of the fads. She wasn't reading the same books as the ladies in our church. She didn't shop at the same stores. In fact, she loved a good thrift-store find.

We both did. Will's mom seemed almost displaced sometimes. Maybe that's why she liked me so much. We both were. She knew it.

Now. Don't get me wrong here. I have nothing against a woman who chooses to make her family and home her sole profession. There are things I love about the idea. It's honorable. It's sacred work. And I know some people who seem genuinely happy and fulfilled in it. My growing concern was more about what I would have to give up to survive in that particular family. The Marley family. My spiritual freedom. My intellectual freedom. My very soul.

***

Golden Streets

I guess one of my biggest problems was the Marleys' God story. The version that I would be expected to believe and help propagate. The version that was so closely intertwined with the branches of the Marleys' family tree. A big part of me becoming a viable branch on that tree required that I teach their story as fact and never question it. *Any* part of it. *Ever.* Will's family, for generations, had been the bodyguards of *the* story. It was untouchable. And I would be required to pass this story down to our children as cold-hard facts—exactly as it was told to me—even the things that I found to be mythical or untrue. And here's the worst part of it: I knew my children also would not be allowed to wonder or challenge without the fear of getting rejected by the Marley tribe. *Their* tribe. Their very own family.

That made my stomach hurt.

Honestly, I can't really remember *not* having my own questions about the nature of God. The pastor we had when I was little told my mother he had never seen a young child listen to a sermon so intently. But what he didn't know was that I never really bought into his sermons. Something felt terribly *off* before I even had the language to say why.

His story and the story of every pastor I had after him went something like this: God is "our father" who loves us more than we could ever imagine. He sent his one and only son as a sacrifice because he really loved him, but he would burn us in hell if we didn't believe it. And here's the really confusing part—Jesus is God's son but also God. And this Jesus, who is really God, would come back one day and take us away from this forsaken trash heap of a world that he, himself, had created in six days only six thousand years ago. Who knows why he even bothered doing that?

Of course, some of us would be raptured into heaven when the damage had gotten to be too great for him to repair. Beamed right up. And he would leave the rest of us abandoned here before we went on permanently to suffer unimaginable pain in our rightful place, burning in hell. *Forever.* Meanwhile, the others who had said they believed the story strolled the golden streets upstairs with no regard for us *down here.* And all that we had to do was say the prayer.

Of course, some denominations say you have to do this thing, the other thing, and that thing too. Some say you even have to keep a running log of any sins and confess them to a priest (male, of course) who had the *only* direct line to the "father." Not us. Not our denomination. We stood by "once saved, always saved." No priest required, at least. And pretty simple. Murder someone? It's cool. Steal a car? No problem. If you sinned, well, "the Devil made you do it." The parables, The Sermon on the Mount? Meh, just suggestions. You say the prayer, and you get into those pearly gates. We called it grace. But you better get that golden ticket, and you better get it in 76.5 years. Because after you croak, time's up. Your grace has expired. And you're screwed. Orphaned forever. Cast into a lake of torturous flames by this father who "loved us so much" only five minutes before we checked out of this dumpster fire of a planet.

So, basically, you see, the whole story hinged on how to stay out of eternal hell "down there." Never mind the hell that we were creating here on Earth. Meh. It's disposable.

Okay. Now. Don't misunderstand me here either. I'm not mocking grace. I'm a believer in grace. I have experienced grace myself. The last ten years have been chock-full of grace, You'll see. I just don't believe that grace runs out. I never did.

Oh. I should also probably mention that even though we were taught that we were worthy of this free golden ticket, we were, at our core, just worthless sinners. The pastor preached Sunday after Sunday that we were, in fact, dirty, wretched, and pretty much helpless. Sometimes even yelling it at us, veins popping out in his neck as he loosened his tie every Sunday mid-sermon. It was like an abusive relationship. He would warmly welcome us with a soft piano piece playing in the background, begin to tear us down about mid-point, give us a hefty tongue-lashing toward the end, and then soothe our wounds as the soft piano cued the altar call.

It was the old wife-beater routine. Black her eye, then bring her a dozen fresh red roses. Strangely, you did have this exhilaration afterwards. The relief of just barely escaping the pits of hell. The "lucky ones." Maybe it's some kind of brain chemistry thing. I don't know. But we went back for more Sunday after Sunday.

I always thought, *Not sure why God even bothered creating such wretchedness. Especially after creating the female. Big mistake there.* The story that my church told was that women were responsible for the whole mess. The garden. The apple. Conspiring with that sneaky talking snake. It was all good before Eve wrecked it. Perfect, in fact. Poor Adam. Tricked. So, the story was that the father would punish *all* women monthly with the pain of menstruation and childbearing. Just a little friendly reminder of her sinful nature. A monthly little slap on the wrist. Why? Because he loved us so much, of course. There is hope for females though. If she kept herself "spotless and pure," she could be redeemed if she was taken in and loved by the superior male—whom she should meekly serve for the rest of her life. Otherwise, pretty clear. She's been possessed. Yep. It's the dreaded "Jezebel spirit."

I always thought that the story needed some serious evaluation. But who was going to be doing any of that? You would be crazy to question an egotistical and psychopathic father like that one. Right? Well, I guess I was just crazy enough. Let me tell you just how crazy before I circle back to Will.

***

Galileo

So, I was just a kid when I armed myself with a community library card. It was the beginning of my seventh-grade year. I had to wait for my mom there after school each day. Their metaphysical section was remarkable for such a small library. I had no interest in boys or drugs. *This.* This was my rebellion. I would sneak onto the back bean bags on the floor of the children's section with my stack. It felt like a secret that only Ms. Margaret, the librarian, and I knew. I started out mainly interested in astronomy. It was my "gateway drug." And I can't really remember the first book that led me to learning more about religious stuff. But as I began researching, I was relieved to learn that I wasn't the only one not buying my church's version of the God story.

On that library floor and over the next several years, whenever and wherever I could find it, I read the words of thinkers that so unapologetically challenged everything that I had been taught from that pulpit. It was my first introduction to the history of the "corporate" church. I read about the Roman Emperor, Constantine, who helped organize the whole religion and got the first group of guys together that played a part in determining what would be in our Bible. The council of Nicaea. The council also came up with our creed. The Nicene Creed. It's basically the corporate mission statement for Christianity.

But Constantine didn't seem to be so "Christ-like." He apparently had his son, brother-in-law, and second wife executed. And some believe he wasn't even really a Christian but saw joining the Christian movement as a way to control the masses. Now, I don't know all of that to be fact, but I think that we could all certainly agree that this "corporate" Christianity set the stage for some abuse of power. Priests and the church were given political clout. And thousands and thousands of people were brutally slaughtered in the name of Jesus. *Jesus.* The guy who said things like "love your neighbor as yourself, the meek shall inherit the Earth, turn the other cheek." You know. *That* guy.

I also read the words of religious scholars who explained how critical pieces of this story had possibly been left out in order to spiritually handicap people. In order to ensure their reliance on the church and priests for the "truth" and their salvation. And to secure their deathbed donations, I guess. In fact, I was surprised to read that many early Christians actually believed in reincarnation and that there may be remnants of it left in books of the Bible. But the whole idea was possibly nixed by the "corporate" church. It's hard to fully control people if they think that they might have another life left in the game, I suppose. And some of the earliest Christian sects, like the Gnostics, recognized Jesus' mission as more of a mystical movement than a religion. But what powerful empire is going to get behind a loosey goosey "mystical" movement?

Also, I read about the "lost books" that were passed over by the councils that created the Bible we have today. So, not really *lost*...but not chosen. Possibly as many as seventy-five books, some, like the Gospel of Thomas, even containing some rather interesting stories about Jesus and some of his more mystical teachings. But I guess the councils didn't see fit for people to have access to *those* stories ... *those* teachings. In fact, the "corporate" church did not want people to have access to any of them without the interference of a priest. I read about William Tyndale, a scholar in the 1500s, who was killed for attempting to translate scriptures for the "common" man. He was charged with "heresy"—strangled and burned at the stake.

Oh. And I discovered that all of this, the history of God Inc., happened just about two seconds ago in the grand scheme of things. The universe is believed to be billions of years old. So, there were billions of years before Jesus, Constantine, or any other "organized" religion came on the scene, including those religions that are older than Christianity.

And I learned we are just a tiny speck in the universe. The universe that contains hundreds of billions of galaxies. Maybe trillions. But if it had been up to corporate Christianity, we might not have ever found that out either. Galileo Galilei, who was a pioneer in astronomy, was put on house arrest by the Catholic church because his findings contradicted the literal interpretation of scripture. The church made a formal apology to him in 1992.

But Galileo wasn't the only one punished for his curious mind. I learned about Rene´ Descartes, a French mathematician and philosopher, who was rumored to have been poisoned by a Catholic priest (with an arsenic-laced communion wafer of all things) due to some of his metaphysical views that didn't mesh with the church. His cause of death is still in question. But I do know that some of his writings were also banned by the church. Just another seeker who sought outside of the hard lines drawn by "corporate" religion and *may* have paid dearly for it. They called them "heretics." I call them heroes.

Apparently, thinking has always been a dangerous business. But I was beyond inspired by these brave thinkers—these heretics. I'm still inspired by them. But at that point in my God story, I was mostly just pissed. Crazy pissed. All the way off. In fact, right off my little hinges.

I felt lied to, manipulated. I felt like we all had been. All the way back. All of us. Jesus had been hijacked. And it was time that someone put a stop to it. And if I couldn't do it, I, at least, didn't want to be a part of it. Okay. Damn me "father" for using the brain you gave me. Damn me straight to hell. I'll enjoy the company of Galileo, Tyndale and the rest of the "heretics" there.

Well ... it's what I wanted to say. But I wasn't quite there yet. What choice did I have in it? I was just a scrawny teenager. If I slept in for Sunday church, I was grounded for three days. Minimum.

***

Jezebel Spirit

The buzz word these days is "deconstruction." I'm not sure who came up with the term. It's basically the dismantling of your formal religious teachings, your God story. I guess my "deconstruction" technically began right there on those bean bags in the corner of the community library, even though my frontal cortex was still just mush.

Meanwhile, I somehow played along. I sang in the youth choir. I went on church mission trips, hayrides, and ski trips. I was in the bell choir. I did the sleep-ins. I went through the motions. But my discoveries that began on that library floor were always right there, bubbling. As you will see, I had many micro-acts of rebellion against my teachings over the next few years. They were satisfying in the moment, but mostly they left me feeling frustrated and rejected. Still, I challenged the tribe. And most dangerously, and probably foolishly, the leaders of the tribe.

Our church believed every story in the Bible to be literal. And it had only one interpretation: *theirs*. I absolutely loved to ask my Sunday school teachers questions like "How did all of the animals possibly fit on Noah's Ark?" I said, "I mean ... there are like six million types of land-dwelling species that have been discovered. There are 5,600 different varieties of land lizards alone." My Sunday school teacher confidently explained that Noah only took the species that had the genetic imprint to populate the Earth with millions of varieties. I said, "Oh! You mean like ... they *evolved*?" Of course, that was a dirty word, "evolution." She, of course, scoffed and the subject was quickly changed, as it often was. But I changed it right back, as I often did.

The questions continued. How did they know the flood covered the Earth if they had not discovered all of it yet? What did the animals eat on the Ark? Each other? Where did they poop? All those animals pooping on a boat, for a *year*? And God tells Noah to take seven pairs but he only took two of each. Did God change his mind about how many? And did Noah and his family just float away watching all the people drown? Babies *drowning*? Noah's son's wives' families *drowning*? They were cool with that? You mean, *God* was cool with that?

Oh, I had the questions. I had lots of questions about the creation story too. Who did Adam and Eve's children marry? And if Adam and Eve didn't know the difference between good and evil before eating the apple, how could they have been expected not to eat the apple? And who named Adam and Eve? And the obvious…a talking snake? Really? If so, what language do snakes use? And what language did Adam and Eve use if they were the first people? And why are there two creation stories? And who wrote either of them down? And there are dinosaur bones around 200 million years old. Did God create dinosaurs? When? And God said "let there be light" at the beginning of Genesis. But he doesn't create the sun until the fourth day. How does that even make sense? And Adam named all the animals? Millions of them? In one day? The dinosaurs too? Were there polar bears in the garden?? Penguins? Did he name all the creatures in the ocean too? How was that even possible? We have only explored like five percent of the ocean. Do you people even know that? And speaking of animals, what about that story where that guy ... Elisha ... has God send bears to maul a bunch of children for making fun of his bald head. Really? God would do that to *children*? For making fun of a bald guy?

And who were these *giants* in Genesis? *Giants*? And who were these "sons of God" who fell in love with the "daughters of man?" I thought Jesus was the only son of God…*and* God too. And if Jesus is God, why does he cry out to God his father in the garden before he was crucified ... and on the cross? Why would he cry out to himself? He *was* God, right? But he calls himself "the son of man" like eighty times in the Bible. What did he even mean? And where even was he between the ages of twelve and thirty something? That's like eighteen years MIA. Seriously? Where was he? Just making furniture? And what happened to his dad? And wait a minute ... after the resurrection, Jesus says that he will return in the disciple's generation. Right? What did he mean? He obviously didn't return. Did he change his mind? Is he ever coming back?

Anyway. You get the picture.

But there was one thing my church was clear about. Crystal clear. My church was utterly obsessed with gay people. Fixated. We had full sermons on it. Of course, no human mind was capable of understanding things like who did Adam and Eve's children procreate with. Nobody could really answer my questions about any of it. But the question of someone being able to love a person of the same sex? Well. That matter was as clear as a bell. We had a few people that regularly picketed gay pride events all over the state. The church praised them for their courage to stand up for God. Sometimes a van full would load up and go. We even took up a collection for a local business that had to shut its doors because it was sued for not providing services to a lady. The church applauded their faithfulness to God's word and family values for refusing to cater a baby shower for the lady's friends, a gay couple.

So, one Sunday, my youth leader made a snarky remark about gay marriage. This was not the first time. Our neighbors and the owner of the market, where I eventually got a job, were gay men, and they had been nothing but kind to me. They had been together longer than I had been alive. So, it struck a nerve.

I felt my face getting hot. I said, "I know a committed gay couple, and they wouldn't appreciate your comments, Brad."

He reached for his Bible and suddenly went from jerky middle school bully Brad to pious young Pastor Brad. "You need to pray for them, Laine. They are living in sin. The Bible is very clear. *Very clear*. For example, the Apostle Paul says ..."

As he was flipping to find the verse, I said, "Oh. The Apostle Paul. Yeah. Wasn't he the one that also very clearly stated that women shouldn't speak in the church?"

He said, "Well, that was cultural. We have to consider the time in which Paul lived." That was probably the wisest thing I ever heard Brad say. But he would eat those words.

I looked at his fiancée standing across the room. They were both students at a local Bible college, and they both had plans for careers in "church planting." Although our church forbade female pastors vehemently, Brad seemed to have his own opinions on *that* particular topic. In fact, his fiancée had just led a very eloquent prayer before we ate.

I said, "Hmmm. Maybe gay marriage is cultural too." He laughed like it was the most ridiculous thing he had ever heard. "Or maybe God changed his mind, like he did on some other things. Like polygamy. Didn't a bunch of guys in the Bible have tons of wives? That's not okay anymore." I continued, "I guess we can all cherry pick the good ol' King James, can't we, Brad?"

The King James Version was the only version of the Bible to be trusted in our church. So, before standing up to take my plate to the kitchen, I decided to twist that knife. I said, "Oh. And speaking of King James, I read he had all kinds of gay lovers. He was quite the player." I stopped and thanked his fiancée, Catherine, for the beautiful prayer.

Yeah. Brad despised me. But I was getting kind of used to being the church Jezebel. It was almost expected of me.

Once our poor minister came to our class to explain communion. He had just come to our church. Fresh meat. Now, our church also forbade alcohol. It was an unspoken rule that the congregation not even frequent a restaurant with a bar. You were sure to be talked about if you were seen even going in one.

So, as he poured the off-brand grape juice, I said, "I have a question." He and the teacher shot eyes at each other. I immediately knew there had been "a meeting." She had obviously clued him in on their budding little Jezebel.

But like a good shepherd, he cautiously said, "Well ... of course, Laine."

I said, "So, why is it that we use grape juice and not wine? I mean, Jesus turned the water into wine in the Bible, at that wedding, right?"

He seemed relieved. He could easily answer this one. "Yes, Laine. His first miracle. The wedding at Cana. But in biblical times, wine was not fermented. You see ... well, it's the fermentation that makes it like the wine that some people drink today." He gently smiled and redirected his attention to the whole class to continue.

He thought he was off the hook. As I casually examined my nails, I said, "So, I have another question."

He looked at the teacher.

The teacher laughed awkwardly and said, "Laine, please, hun ... just ... just let the pastor finish ... 'kay?"

I said, "Oh, okay. I was just going to say that it was interesting to me that it was unfermented grape juice. But wasn't Jesus even accused of being a drunkard because he drank wine? Didn't they call him a 'glutton and a drunkard' or something like that? Anyway, I guess you can get drunk on unfermented grape juice. Fill my cup to the top then!" My classmates snickered. A few glared.

I didn't care either way. Mission accomplished. Laine 548–Brainwashers 0.

His wife pulled me from class not long after that. She was going to give me a "gentle" correction. She needed help with a bulletin board. It obviously had been pre-arranged.

As we stapled these paper snowflakes onto bright blue construction paper, I remember her saying, "Laine, I hear you are quite inquisitive."

I shrugged. "I guess so."

Then she said, "Baby, you just have to have faith." She stopped, grabbed me by the shoulders and repeated in about five strung out syllables "Faaiittth."

I felt my body go completely stiff as she hugged me. I said, "Faith in what?"

She said, "Well, God, of course, honey."

I said, "I do. What makes you think I don't?"

"Well, your teacher says you don't seem to believe any of the stories. These are beautiful stories given to us as a gift. It is the word of God, Laine." Smiling, trying to hide her scorn, she said again slowly, "It is the word of God, baby girl."

I stopped what I was doing and looked at her. "So, what you are saying is God told people to write down these stories word for word. Right? Word for word. All of them?"

A look of relief flashed across her face. She nodded her head and smiled. "Yeeesss." She put her hands on my shoulders again.

I said, "Hmmm. Interesting. Well, first of all ... it wasn't recorded in American English thousands of years ago. You do know that. Right? There are thousands of translations. And some guys—yes, just guys—decided which books would be in there. And even if the translation of *those* books is even *close* to accurate, are stories always literal? The stories Jesus told weren't always literal. Were they? The parables. Maybe God didn't intend for you to read some of his stories literally either. Also, if this Bible is the literal word of God, he might want to get his story straight."

Her eyes narrowed. Her lips pursed. She firmly said, "Laine, now, we are not going to judge the word of God right here in His house. You are on holy ground, child."

I proceeded to staple the snowflakes. "Oh, I'm just making an observation. Mathew, Mark, Luke, and John didn't even agree on the order of how some things happened. And the Apostle Paul's teachings don't really even line up with what *Jesus* taught. There are contradictions all over the place. Google it yourself."

She was getting ready to set the whole internet straight about that. She said, "You can't trust —"

I interrupted her. "You know what? Here's the deal. You people seem to worship that book more than you do the God you say wrote it. In fact, it seems to me that you have him trapped in the pages of it. Do you really believe *the* God that created this whole universe could fit neatly into *one* little book? And do you really believe *our* church has the one and *only* correct translation and interpretation? Maybe you are the one who needs to have some faith, baaabbby girl. It seems to me you worship a book, not God. And, *yes,* we *are* on holy ground. *That* is why this insanity needs to stop. It's gone on way too long. Two thousand years too long." I handed her the stapler and walked back into the classroom.

As I did, I heard her murmur, "What a stupid little bitch."

Inerrancy was their idol. It was their golden calf. And they would do anything to defend it. No surprise. That next Sunday, the sermon was on what appeared to be biblical "errors" that weren't errors at all. The pastor explained that the "discrepancies" were "divinely *allowed* to set a snare for the doubters and unbelievers." I thought, *First of all, there was definitely a conversation at their dinner table last Sunday night. And secondly, wow. Just wow.* But I have to say, the mental gymnastics were impressive. *So, let me get this straight. Snares? Add trickster to this abusive father's good attributes. Why would a loving father trick us? Because he loves us so much, of course.* I thought, *Just check your brain at the door, people. Just check it at the door. It won't be needed here.*

That morning, I sat there between my parents with my arms tightly crossed, refusing to bend, glaring. Are my parents even hearing this nonsense? *Do they even care?* Honestly, they didn't. I regret to say my parents were just happy to be ticket holders. That sermon or any other sermon was never discussed or dissected on the way home or at lunch afterwards. In fact, we rarely talked about God at home.

My dad had grown up in that church, but my parents were just consumers. Members. This was a social event. Another morning at the club. And for whatever reason, I never challenged them about it. I guess it was because they never shoved it down my throat like the pastor's wife. Sometimes, I thought, *What if I had Jezebel parents who were also shaking their fists, raging at the religious machine? What would that even look like? Or even worse, what if I had parents who taught this insanity at home? Trickster God theology.* Either scenario sounded nightmarish. I realized I probably had gotten the right parents.

Anyway, I was the wet blanket. I was the party crasher too. The Sunday before Christmas, one of the teachers brought a big, white sheet cake. In red and green icing were the words HAPPY BIRTHDAY JESUS! We lit candles. The kids were buzzing around, high on Christmas excitement and icing. As I was licking the icing off my fork, I said, "You guys do know Jesus wasn't really born on December 25th, don't you? Theologians say it was most likely in the fall. There was some Pagan god born on December 25th. Constantine just stole the day from the Pagans. He stole the whole Christmas tree thing from them too."

I was just getting started raining on this happy little parade when my classmate, John, pushed up his glasses, looked at me, and said, "Theologians? What are those? And Constant who? Never mind. You know what? Who even cares, Laine? Why don't you just shut up for once in your life?" He rolled his eyes and dug into his cake. I thought to myself that time ... and many times ... *I wish I didn't care. God, help me. I wish I didn't. I wish I could just be satisfied with my birthday cake and my golden ticket.*

I'm sure my Sunday school teachers loved it when our family went away for the weekend. Who could blame them, right?

I did have one Sunday school teacher I will never forget. Mrs. McCracken. I think it was the beginning of my tenth-grade year. I didn't antagonize her. I mean, I attempted to once. I asked her about the billions of galaxies that had been discovered with the Hubble telescope. I asked something like, "Why did God just put life on one tiny planet in such a ginormous universe? And scientists have discovered that the universe is expanding, but that's not in the creation story. So, is God still creating? Why doesn't the Bible talk about that?" Normally, I would have gotten an answer intended to plant seeds of doubt in these "secular" ideas that were not to be trusted under any circumstances. Like, are there actually all these galaxies? How do we know the universe is expanding? Or the favorite go-to, "There are just things that our human minds can't understand, Laine." Basically, we shouldn't even try. And scientists? Pffffft. Well, they were doing the Devil's work. They were all atheists. Of course, all scientists believed we came straight from dirty monkey DNA. All of them. But Mrs. McCracken didn't believe that. I remember her eyes got really big. Her face lit up. And almost with a giddiness, she said, "Ohhhh Laine! I wonder the same kinds of things sometimes!" I knew my curiosity was safe with her. I loved her class. I missed three Sundays in a row one time.

I got a Valentine in the mail that read:

> *Laine!*
> *We have missed your light so much!*
> *I hope you are enjoying this snow.*
> *Happy Valentine's Day.*
> *You are so very loved.*

XOXO
Mrs. McCracken

I thought, *My light? What light? So very loved? Mrs. McCracken made me want to be good.*

Anyway, I guess you are wondering about now how Will, the prince of the kingdom, hooked up with the mouthy, obnoxious church Jezebel.

Okay. Back to Will.

***

Girl Problems

I guess one saving grace was that the girls and boys were separated a lot of the time. I assume they wanted minimal intermingling before marriage. And girls had different "expectations" to follow that required an extra-large dose of brainwashing. Like how to stay "pure" enough so we could only be chosen one day. Of course, that was our sole purpose. Will didn't see Jezebel in "action" very often. And the Marleys traveled quite a bit. He was rarely there. And, well, I guess I'm not a homely girl. I mean, I had been a tomboy most of my life. But my junior year, I had learned to do my makeup and fix my hair. In fact, my hair had become my crowning glory, thick and wavy, almost to my waist. Everybody always thought I paid for expensive highlights. I got voted "Best Mane" in our fake superlatives our Senior year. So, I had a bit of a "glow up," I guess. And, honestly, I had dialed Jezebel way back by this time. Maybe that year in Mrs. McCracken's class had that effect on me. But that was the year, eleventh grade. The year that boys began to notice me — in a good way now. Will definitely did.

So, like I said, Will and I began dating the summer after our junior year. We both joined the puppet team, mainly so neither of us had to sing in the choir. We spent hours in close quarters practicing puppeteering. Then, after that trip to Maryland, he kissed me on the back stairwell of the church, and we were official.

Our senior year was a blur. One magical head-spinning blur. On most weekends, I worked at Ivy's Market. Will would come there to bring me yummy food. Any reason to see me. We had prom, graduation parties, banquets, and senior trip. And, of course, all of our church events and responsibilities. I was booked, busy, and happy. *Very happy.* I felt like I belonged. I was accepted, even chosen. I have to admit, it felt nice. I thought, *Maybe I could settle into this kind of life. Maybe I was even wrong about some things. Maybe none of it really mattered anyway. Maybe my Jezebel spirit had been loved right out of me.*

But by the end of that next summer after graduation, things began to cool off. The chemicals settled down, I guess. The staying up half the night on the phone began to become less and less frequent. The spontaneous pop-ins at the market became nonexistent. Will started spending more time with his friends. Golf became his new passion. His new love interest. Yet, I knew he was in for the long haul. His mother had taken me in as one of her own. His sister and I had become friends.

And we— should I dare say— had "fornicated." So, the deal was basically signed, sealed, and delivered despite the fact that our church spent a great deal of time ensuring this would never happen. Well, like I said, with the girls anyway. We had a ceremony when we were in "Girls in Grace" at around twelve. We all wore a white dress and made a promise to God to keep ourselves pure until marriage. Our dads would walk us down the aisle to the pastor who would give us a certificate, and we would go stand in a line in front of the church for the congregation to stare at us. Kind of creepy if you think about it. I developed a violent cough the morning of my ceremony. It *mysteriously* disappeared that afternoon.

Anyway, purity was another obsession in my church. I remember when Will and I had been dating for about three months, we were sitting with the youth group in the balcony. At the altar call, our pastor began talking to us all directly. The parents turned around to look at us up there, making sure we were paying attention or trying to read our faces for signs of guilt. Either way, soon the whole congregation's attention was on us. He then asked us to come down to the front for prayer if we had fornicated and needed forgiveness or wanted to make a commitment to our continued purity. One or the other. That would cover all the bases.

So, he stood there expecting us to file in line down the aisle to the front. Like a mid-puberty purity recommitment ceremony, I guess. But we all sat there like deer in headlights. Now, Will and I had not fornicated—yet. But it was still the most interesting conundrum. And I looked down the pew at the rest of the youth and those in the row in front of us, and, well, let's just say there was a whole herd of deer in headlights. And let's also say, about a third of them were known to be long-time fornicators. Like *professional ones.* They knew who they were, and they knew we all knew who they were, so we all just sat there in an alliance.

***

The Prince and the Pond Frog

It had once seemed impossible to leave Will for school. But, when the time came, I was ready. I was headed for a university that was an eleven-hour drive from home. Will finally decided to stay behind to go to an in-state school. Of course, we kept up appearances. We maintained our social media image. We traveled a couple of times for visits. We texted throughout the day, talked on the phone every night.

But by Christmas, our conversations had grown dull and lifeless for the most part. I was doing a lot of reading and learning again. Lots of *Jezebel* kinds of things. Science was not just my major, it was my passion. And I was also learning on my own about alternative medicine, nutrition, herbs. I tossed around the idea of medical school, except I thought I would meet the same dogma in the medical community I had met in my church. I mean, seriously, they were open to new ideas but only if there was a dollar sign firmly attached to them.

I tried to share ideas with Will, thinking, maybe if we read some books together, maybe that would breathe some life back into all of this. It didn't. Like I said, Will was smart. Wicked smart in his own way. But he had zero curiosity about anything that didn't affect him directly. He was beyond uninterested in all my discoveries and latest epiphanies. His indifference was growing as was my dissatisfaction.

In my soul, I knew this chapter was coming to a close. It needed to come to a close. It was past time. But I couldn't admit it to myself, or him, or our mothers, who were probably back home looking at wedding venues and double strollers. So, I guess that I began, almost subconsciously, pushing him away. I started making passive-aggressive remarks about his family, his golf obsession, his beliefs. Actually, I don't even know if Will had beliefs of his own. I guess I was attacking his family's beliefs that he was unwilling to challenge me.

I had morphed right back into little Miss Jezebel in Sunday school class, challenging the big bad Sunday School regime. But this time, I met worse than frustration. I met apathy.

Will avoided confrontation like the plague. He always did. I realize now it was probably a coping skill he developed to survive his father. But there was never any attempt to challenge my ruthless attacks or unpack why I might be acting so differently than the mostly carefree Laine that had left for school in the fall. Just polite conversation and empty goodnights. Scripted sign offs like, "Get some rest, Laine. Hopefully, you will feel better tomorrow." For Will, thinking was just some kind of illness one needed to recover from. All I heard through his indifference was "Just follow the script, Laine, please. For God's sake, just follow the damn script."

I feel bad about how I treated Will during those months. Honestly. He was beyond patient with me. And it wasn't his fault. I once read "You can't talk ocean language with a pond frog." I don't know who said it.

But Will was a happy little pond frog. There's nothing inherently wrong with being a pond frog. I suppose pond frogs are a critical part of the ecosystem. And who could blame him for not wanting to be anything else? His life had been a pond frog's dream.

But I craved more. I wanted to swim in the deepest depths of the bluest oceans. I always had big questions. And it wasn't my fault either. It's who I was, an ocean dweller. I had always been. I had always pressed for answers. Of course, did I really want the answers to my Sunday school questions? Could anyone even answer them if I did? I didn't really care if there were 5,600 land lizards on Noah's Ark. Or if Adam named every one in a single day? I didn't even care if the stories were true at all. My faith wasn't in the stories. My faith was in a God of an unimaginably vast and beautiful universe. And I wanted freedom. I, at least, wanted the right to have questions brought into the light to be examined without being punished, ridiculed or ostracized by the tribe for it. I thought, *God gave me this brain, dammit.* And I wasn't a little girl on the floor of the library. I had deeper, more consequential questions now.

I so desperately wanted a comrade in Will. I really did. Instead, I had this pond frog. Adorable. Sweet. Comfortable. Apathetic. Pond frog.

Chapter 2

Linguine

By Spring break, I didn't even want to go home. By summer break, I didn't plan to, but the living arrangements I had made fell through when my roommate transferred to a school closer to her home. And Will's dad offered me a summer job in the "marketing department "of his firm. Well, his mom did. She arranged the whole thing. But they were expanding to a nearby town. It made sense they would soon need some fresh ideas for marketing material. This business had been built on "who you know" for generations, not any flashy advertising. I was told that Mr. Marley was willing to look at something new, but I knew he might not want to reinvent the wheel. It was obviously working just fine at the first office. Marketing wasn't my major, but I guess Will's mom knew I was kind of creative and a little bit tech savvy, compared to their dinosaur staff anyway. And I did need something besides Ivy's Market on my nonexistent résumé. So, I packed up my things and my bad attitude, and I headed home.

Home felt strange at first. When I went home for short breaks, my schedule was so jam packed that my room was just a place for wardrobe changes. But now I would be home for over two months. My parents treated me like a visitor. The nagging to get my laundry done turned into a stack of fresh towels on my bed. Nobody expected me to feed Gus or change the litter box. I had no curfew. My mom would open my bedroom door to say hello and just awkwardly stare. At first, I preferred to be at Mr. Marley's office, and I was kind of excited by the challenges.

They were literally in the Stone Ages with a lot of their technology and systems. I was flooded with ideas for them. And my not-really-so-genius ideas were met with amazement by Betty, the unofficial (and untitled) director of marketing, and the rest of the office staff. It didn't take much to impress her. Betty had been there a million and a half years. She was just tired and grateful for the help. I felt like a marketing wizard. And Will's dad was working in the new office two hours away the first two weeks I was there. And he was in Italy, with Will's mom, for the next three. I didn't have the pressure of performing for him. *All in all, not a bad gig,* I thought.

The month or so before Mr. Marley was back, we got tons done. We were like kids at play. Betty was just delighted at anything and everything we did. I would bring fresh bagels every morning. And she would take me out to lunch at the country club or the swanky little Italian restaurant a block over. She would brag about me to anyone she saw that she knew and gush about Will, her "Ginger Baby." Betty loved Will. Everybody in the office loved Will. She would stretch out lunch as long as she could just bragging and telling me stories about all of the parties and locally "famous" people she had met in this job and the job she had at the bank before she came to work for the Marleys in her thirties. I never felt guilty about lunch because we almost always worked a little late. I even took work home some nights. But Betty and I were having one heck of a time. I thought, *If this is work, I will never retire.*

But it was short lived. I noticed as the days grew closer to when Mr. Marley was supposed to be back in our office, Betty was different and growing kind of anxious, uptight. The whole staff was, really. The receptionist began obsessively cleaning. I left my mug of tea and my bag from the bagel shop on her desk one morning. She bit my head off. She told me we tried to keep the front of the office "presentable" and if I wouldn't mind helping to keep it that way by not leaving my "trash" up there. I thought, *Did that really just happen? Was I just scolded by Tammy? Sweet Tammy?* Jim, one of the older accountants in the office, also suddenly became curt with me. Once jovial, always good for some small talk in the mail room, he became quiet and dismissive.

We weren't having fun anymore. *Maybe the honeymoon is just over,* I thought. But the newness had worn off pretty quickly. *Maybe this was their normal. And maybe this is why people just want to make it until Friday in these office jobs. Maybe this is why people just beg for early retirement.*

But it made more sense when Betty and I went to lunch one last time. Some of it anyway.

She said, "Okay, there's something you really need to know, Laine." Nervously, her eyes were darting around like we were in the mafia or something. "When Mr. Marley is in town, things are different. They have to be different."

"Ummm ... different ... like how so?"

"Well, Laine ... Mr. Marley likes things a certain way. Like lunches. This is normally a special occasion thing. You know, it's a birthday kind of thing."

I didn't understand. We always had paid for our own. And even if we hadn't, we would split a dish if we wanted something "heavy on our bellies" as Betty would call it. It's not like we were out having crab legs and caviar on the company every day.

I said, "What's the problem, Betty?"

"He just doesn't like it. It's the principle of it, I guess."

"You mean it's morally wrong to split a pasta dish on a plain old Tuesday? Well, it isn't for him. He is in

Florence today for God's sake. I wonder what he's having for lunch? I guess the commoners live differently though. Is that how it is, Betty?"

She looked away for a second. Her eyes settled on the front door where a well-dressed couple was being greeted overzealously by the hostess. She knew that was exactly how it was. "Trust me. It's better just to keep him happy. I don't know. I mean ... there are lots of things he just does and doesn't like. Too many things to really tell you about." Her shoulders dropped. She put her fork down, her pasta barely eaten. "When he comes back, just follow my lead. Just trust me on this."

I thought, *Are we talking about the same Bill Marley? Will's dad? I mean ... I never got the warm fuzzies from the guy, but she's acting like we could be executed out back for messing up the printer or something.*

What Betty didn't know was that I was growing kind of tired of her "Ginger Baby." The Marley family, this town—the whole God-forsaken scene. And Betty had only seen my nice side. She had never met Jezebel. We had basically been running the show on a carb-induced high of fresh bagels and linguine. She didn't know that I wasn't really "one of them." I had played along for one summer too many. All I had to lose at this point was a good reference and a lukewarm relationship with the owner's son. She thought I was going to keep playing nice. Anything to keep Mr. Marley happy. Anything to keep the peace in his miserable little kingdom. Not this little Jezebel. Not for long.

The Marleys returned from their trip. That Sunday, I spoke to Mr. Marley briefly in the parking lot after church. Forced yet cordial conversation. No surprises.

"So. How was Italy?"

"Fantastic. Betty said you have been working hard."

"Trying to. We've gotten a lot done."

"That's good. See you tomorrow."

I thought, *Yep, same vanilla guy I've known most of my life.*

I was half anxious and half eager to see this three-headed monster emerge that Betty warned me about.

***

Last Will and Testament

On Monday morning I coached myself as I was getting ready. *You can do this. It's just a few weeks. It will be over before you know it.* I stopped by the bagel shop. I got my cinnamon and Betty's blueberry. But when I got in the car, I realized I had forgotten the cream cheese. I thought, *I'm pushing it on time. Oh well.* I headed back into the shop. There stood one of my mom's friends. I stopped to chat. I remembered she had sent me a graduation card and a fifty in it. I hadn't seen her since leaving for college. What choice did I have? I got back in my car. *Dammit! It is after eight o'clock. No. Not on the first day that the warden is back.*

I walked in, and Tammy just looked at me. She looked at her watch ostentatiously while spinning her chair around to open a filing drawer. Then back at me. I was still holding on to my grudge about the bagel bag scolding. I sarcastically said, "Oh! look at you already multitasking so early in the morning." Eye roll. The office was eerily quiet. My heels sounded like they were echoing as I walked down the hallway. I had never realized how long it was, and every step was painfully loud. Betty wasn't in her office. It looked like nobody was in their office. I went to my desk and opened emails as I ate my bagel. I felt guilty for even having it. I thought, *Are commoners even allowed bagels on plain old Mondays?*

Around nine thirty, Betty popped into my office. She said, "Mr. Marley wants us to outline what we have done in the boardroom this afternoon. All of the managers are going to be here. Can you do a two o'clock?" I replied, "Sure. I'll be there." *What else did I have to do*? No mention of lunch. No idle chit-chat. She ignored the bag from the bagel shop and just disappeared back into her office. I spent most of the morning reading the news on my laptop. No more collaboration or stories. No more linguine. Betty was doing whatever she normally did before me. It was unclear exactly what my job was for the next few weeks. I skipped lunch.

Finally, two o'clock rolled around. Betty dropped by to get me. She said, "I've already shown Mr. Marley our ideas. Just bring a legal pad and take notes." I tore off the first few pages of the one on my desk where I had been doodling, grabbed a pen, and followed Betty to the other side of the building where Mr. Marley's office and the boardroom were located.

Behind the heavy wooden door, it felt like the lobby of a funeral home. Fake plants. Fake gothic columns. And outdated mauve and green floral prints. There was stale coffee still in the pot next to a stack of small Styrofoam cups. She told me to grab a cup if I wanted. *A special treat for the peasants?* I rolled my eyes and said, "I'll pass." Betty sat three chairs down from the head of the table. I sat across from her. The whole vibe was beyond strange. I felt like someone was getting ready to read someone's last will and testament.

Then, coming down the hall, I heard Mr. Marley's voice along with some other male voices. One was Jim's. They entered. An entourage of cheap suits. Mr. Marley glanced at me. He offered everyone the stale coffee. One politely took him up on it. Then, the three men—and Jim—took the seats closest to the head of the table where Mr. Marley sat. No introductions. I suddenly never existed.

So, here we were at our meeting about the work Betty and I had done over the last month. We were seated the farthest from Mr. Marley. We gave him our best, and all the guy had to offer us was a stale cup of coffee. We sat awkwardly. Finally, after reading and responding to a text, he spoke. "Okay let's knock this out." I remembered Betty saying, "Just follow my lead." I waited. Mr. Marley said, "So, Betty showed me the new marketing materials at our staff meeting this morning, and we need to decide if this is something we can use for here and the new office." Betty slid a folder toward him. He took out my brochures, my logo proposals, my hard work and placed it in the middle of the table. The men—and Jim—who actually knew me just a short week ago, look and nod. Indifferent. The one guy was still trying to get his powdered creamer stirred into his coffee. Nobody asked to see the work I had done on the website or the new social media pages. There was not even a laptop to be found in the room. I felt like I had been teleported back in time. And I couldn't get out of there quickly enough. I needed fresh air. I needed sunlight. *Use the materials ... or not. I'm not going to be around to find out.* I excused myself to "the restroom." On the way out that afternoon, I threw Betty's bagel in the trash can in her office.

I continued to watch the office staff morph into some robotic version of themselves. Betty barely spoke. I felt partially betrayed and partially sorry for them. I never even saw Mr. Marley. He wasn't the three-headed monster. He barely existed. He stayed on the other side of the building—in the funeral quarters.

***

Freedom

I vowed to make the best of my remaining weeks there. I volunteered for any errands. Any excuse to get out into the sunshine. I was still studying nutrition. I had become a bit of a health nut that first year at school. I began bringing interesting lunches. A mid-morning snack. An early-afternoon snack. Carefully packed. Big colorful salads, Brazil nuts, clementines, fresh berries, coconut milk yogurt, apples with cashew butter and raw honey, boiled farm fresh eggs with coarse Himalayan sea salt—just the right amount. And I brought my favorite mug and drank oolong tea with squares of dark chocolate in the afternoon. I painted my nails a fresh color every few days. I made a travel inspiration board on Pinterest and started reading "The Tao of Pooh." A simple little read, an introduction to the age-old philosophy of Taoism, otherwise known as "the Devil's work" in that town.

I often brought a change of clothes and ran the greenway along the river in the historic district after work—even before Mr. Marley came back. Will would join me if he wasn't working on his golf game. I ran by the old homes I had always loved growing up. Most, if not all, had been restored. It was nearing the Fourth of July. Many of the homes were decked out in red, white, and blue bunting flags on that day—that day Will and I fought. Well, we didn't *fight*. I should say the day neither of us even cared enough to fight. The day I knew I wouldn't spend one more summer with Will Marley.

I had always loved the Fourth of July. Our town had an old-fashioned celebration downtown every year. All the kids decorated their bikes. There was a marathon. A dog show. Sack races. There was a waterslide up on Monument Hill—we didn't think it strange at all that on the other side of the hill were the graves of soldiers who had died. Symbolic really. If you think about it. There was any kind of summertime food you could want. Hamburgers, BBQ, funnel cakes, corn dogs. Every church in town had a booth. Our church made slices of homemade cake. All kinds. They always melted in the sun by two o'clock, sticking to the plastic wrap, just goo by the end of the day. But it's what we did. Every year. And I loved it.

After our run that day, we were cooling down at our cars and talking about our plans for the Fourth. Somehow,

I was genuinely excited to spend the whole day with Will despite the lack of "fireworks." And I didn't intend to jab or demean him. It was totally innocent. But I said something like, "I think I really love the Fourth of July because of what it represents. You know ... freedom." He looked away. No interest. If nothing else, I was going to at least complete my thought. I said, "Yeah ... freedom. Think about it. People risked their lives to come to this country. Like for freedom of worship. Of course, the Catholics had persecuted the Protestants but funny how the Protestants then began persecuting the Catholics when they got here. Weird, huh? At least we don't do witch hunts or hang people in the streets anymore, I guess. Progress is progress. Oh! You want to know what I read the other day?"

Will slowly and almost methodically wiped the sweat off his forehead with the bottom of his T-shirt. Then, finally, he put his hands on his hips. He lowered his head to look me straight in the eye and said, like he'd been dying to say it his whole life, "No. I don't really want to know, Laine. But I'm one hundred and ten percent sure you are going to tell me." It took me a second to switch gears. I said almost nervously, "Oh ... oh ... okay ... never mind then. Forget I even asked."

In that moment, a part of me wanted so badly for him to say something like, "I'm sorry, Laine. I'm genuinely interested. Please tell me what you read." Part of me wanted him to pull me in for one of those hugs. Maybe tease me. I'd make him beg me to tell him. Instead, he said, emotionless, as he unlocked his car, "Going to Jeb's tonight to watch the game. I'll call you when I get home." No interest. Apathy. After he drove away, I just stood there.

His words echoed in my head. "No. I don't really want to know." I thought, *You don't ... do you? You don't want to know anything more than what you already know. And you never will.* Of course, I knew that I couldn't play victim. My plan to push him away had been fully and completely executed. This was what I wanted. It's what my soul wanted. Freedom. I had long outgrown this pond.

That night, my phone buzzed. I didn't answer. And he didn't bother to leave a message. There was nothing left to say. Not one solitary word. It settled into a kind of truce. A mutual ghosting, I guess. I was just numb. And he was just interested in shaving some strokes off his game—or so I thought.

***

Delilah

The office was closed the day before the Fourth. Mr. Marley let the church youth use his back lot for the vendors that were setting up downtown. He charged twenty dollars per space, and the money went to the youth's fall trip. So, I used the day to do some self-care and to catch up with a couple of friends. We met for coffee and hit a thrift shop. It was really good to see them. Much needed. I was safe to be silly. I wanted to spend all day in their familiarity. But I had made a one o'clock hair appointment weeks before. My friends agreed that a long, angled bob would give me a fresh look. A "lob" they called it. So, a "lob" it would be.

I had photos on my phone to show the stylist exactly what I wanted. I had randomly chosen her. The salon was high-end. Their products smelled like heaven. The salon served this hot fennel tea I just loved. It was definitely a splurge. But I had barely spent any of the money I had made that summer. I got a wash, scalp massage, and a deep conditioning treatment. It felt so good to be pampered. Then, finally, I was in the master's chair. I showed her the photos. She crinkled up her nose. Shrugged. Said something like, "What's the point?" She went and got some hair magazines. Flipped through them. She said, "Shoot ... I thought I had it dog-eared. Let me look at this other one." I waited. I tried not to look at myself in the mirror. Hair slicked back. My morning makeup now smeared. The concealer completely gone from the crater in my forehead. And the damn cape— practically strangling me. *Ugh. Just get on with it.*

Then, who I will call Delilah finally returned and said, "Oh, oh, here ... here it is. You are going to love it!" Like it was already decided. "Your face shape is absolutely perfect for it. Perfect." Her excitement. Who could resist? For some reason, these situations always cripple me. I looked at the photo in the magazine. I said sheepishly, "Well ... I mean ... it's short. Really short. I mean ... I've never had my hair that short. Maybe in the fifth grade." I tried to muster up the courage. I said, "Well, it's gorgeous on her. I mean ... but she's gorgeous." I struggled to find an escape. A way out. But I didn't want to disappoint her. She was so excited. Passionate even. And it's just hair, right?

"Okay. Let's go for it."

What's the quote? "A girl who is going to cut her hair is getting ready to change her life." That's not it. Something like that.

My hair is super thick. So, first she pulled it into three wet pigtails. I was still trying to avoid the mirror. She took a phone call. *Are you kidding me? Right now?* I had this sudden urge to jerk that cape off and run.

That's ridiculous. Ugh. I waited. She finally hung up, and, in a flash, pulled out her scissors and cut off each bunch of hair just above each clear elastic rubber band while telling me about her plans for the remodel of the 1930's bungalow she had just bought and what her electrician told her on the phone.

Snip, snip, snip.

My hair. Within seconds, my crowning glory lay in three bunches on the floor. And she barely even stopped talking long enough to scoop them up, walk them over to the trash can, and dump them like useless dead bodies. She returned like nothing ever happened. I heard all about her custom cabinets while she went to work shaping it into the cut in the magazine—kind of—I guess. A cousin of it anyway. I attempted to interject casually into the conversation like part of my soul wasn't just sitting over there in the trash can. But I finally surrendered. I just closed my eyes, settled into my chair, and let her blow it dry.

When she was finished, she grabbed my shoulders and said, "You ready for a look?" Handed me a mirror and spun me around. I thought, W*ow ... yep ... it's definitely gone.* Then, she spun me around to the front as she somehow simultaneously removed my cape. All I could see were my blue eyes against the pale blue T-shirt I chose that morning. Even with the smudged mascara, they looked bluer. Clearer somehow. I paused. I took a deep breath. Handed her the mirror. "I like it."

I returned to an empty house, obsessively looking in the bathroom mirror. Took a few selfies. Redid my makeup. Full face of it. Earrings. No earrings. More selfies. I really did like it. I thought, *I may even love it.*

I found out my parents were at a work function for Dad. I fixed myself a sandwich, took a bath, washed all my makeup off, and got into my bed. For a second, I thought about sending Will a message. Muscle memory, I guess. I scrolled mindlessly on my phone, and soon, I was out cold. I heard my parents come in the front door. *Geez, what time is it?* By the time I found my phone to check, my mom was popping her head in the doorway.

"Hey, Elaina Elaine ... did you get dinner? We have leftovers from the restaurant." She only called me that when she was in a super good mood.

Slightly disoriented from the heavy sleep, I forgot I had even cut my hair. Rubbing my eyes, I sat up in my bed.

She looked closer. "Laine?"

I said, "Oh. I heard you ... I'm awake, I'm awake. And no thanks. I had a sandwich."

She continued. "No, Laine ... your hair."

"Ohhh ... yeah ... I cut it today. Putting my hands beneath my chin, cocking my head and batting my eyelashes, I said, "Well? What do ya think?" No response.

I had trouble reading the look on her face. *Was it sadness? No. It's disappointment ... with a dose of anger.*

"You don't like it?"

As she was shaking off her true feelings about it, she said, "Well ... does Will like it?" Like that would redeem me if he did.

I said, "I don't know. I haven't even talked to him since Friday." If the haircut didn't do it, this surely did.

"What do you mean?"

"I mean I haven't talked to Will since last Friday, and honestly, I don't know if I will ever speak to him again."

Oh. I had done it. Her only child. Her one shot. Now, a complete disappointment.

I remember now ... it was Coco Chanel who said it. "A woman who cuts her hair is about to change her life."

***

Bumblebee

The next day I woke up with the sudden realization that I had made plans with Will weeks before for the Fourth of July. We had signed up to man the church booth from noon until two o'clock. I thought, *I can't make that the first time we speak again. What if we hash it out right there in the church booth? That can't happen. Maybe I just don't go. That would be the Jezebel thing to do. Just go full rogue. Maybe I can find a replacement? The less Jezebel thing to do. Ugh.* I grabbed my phone. Texted casually like I wasn't in a serious relationship with this guy less than a week ago. "Hey, Will. Are you still working at the booth tomorrow?" No response. *Maybe I should just call him. This is so bizarre.* Finally, he replied, "No. Gracie is covering for me." Even worse in some ways. Grace Anne—his sister. She would have questions. Or ... she would already know. I didn't know which was worse. I just stared at my phone. No follow up of where he would be instead. Not even a "How are you?" Nothing.

You know, there's this weird thing when you break up with someone, isn't there? You are relieved on one hand. At the very same time, a part of you just wants things back to normal. Stat. Like the daily micro-miseries of staying in the relationship are easier than the big blast of misery getting out of it. It feels like death. It is a death. A death of a future once imagined. In this case, it was the death of a lot of things ... my relationship with my first love, my parents' hopes and dreams for me, my relationship with Will's mom, my relationship with his sister, the little Marleys that would never be born. And the death of the version of my future self that would be buried alongside all of it. Grief is work. I heard someone say once, "You can't go around grief. You have to go straight through it. There are no detours."

I sat there looking at my phone. *Is he just sitting there staring at his too? What is he doing? Where is he? I hate this.* Everything felt wrong — like a hollow homesick feeling. Finally, I decided. *Not today. I can't. I'm not going around it— or through it. Not today anyway. I'll just undo it. I'll be good. I'll follow the script. Maybe forever. I don't know. But right now, I'm not ready for this. And I mean, really, who could want more. It's William J. Marley IV for God's sake. I have to undo this. I want my old life back.*

But I wasn't going to be chasing a boy. I'm a Southern girl. And no Southern girl is going to just hand herself right over.

You draw them in. "You are the flower. They are the bumblebee," my Gram used to say. "Flowers don't chase. They just have to stand there in their beauty."

I got up the next morning. I thought, *Will may not be working at the booth. But sometime between the race and the fireworks, I know I'll see him.* I got ready like it was prom. My hair was still good and still smelled like the herbal products she used at the salon. I took a long bath. I exfoliated, did a clay mask. Painted my nails red. Placed spoons in the freezer for my puffy eyes. I found my favorite white cutoffs in the laundry. They were basically clean. I tried on no less than four shirts. I settled in on a soft faded navy-blue T-shirt. I never wore eyeshadow. But I used a little. Not too much. I scrubbed my lips with my toothbrush to make them a little plump. Plumping lip gloss. Gargled with mouthwash. More lip gloss. More mouthwash.

It was eleven o'clock. It was an hour before I had to be at the booth. My stomach was in knots. I heard cheering. It was the marathon runners coming over the finish line one by one. I walked over to watch them. I saw a few people I knew from school running. I clapped. Waved. Cheered them on to the finish. Then, I turned my head to see who was coming up over the hill. It was him. It was like a sighting of a celebrity crush. My stomach tightened. I worked my way over to the finish line. *I'll just happen to be there. I'll hug him—sweat and all. Just congratulating him, of course. He will pull me in tightly. So glad to see me. We will laugh at ourselves. The ridiculousness of it all. He will love the smell of my hair and tell me how cute the cut is on me. It's all good. Just a few more minutes, and this will all be behind us. Just a temporary lapse of insanity. That's all.*

But as he was coming closer, I noticed he was keeping perfect pace with someone. A girl. A girl with a long brown ponytail swaying from side to side. Athletic but feminine body. She was beautiful. She was a runner too. I could tell. Will's type. I stopped. *Wait. What's happening here? Maybe it's just a fluke. Maybe they just happen to be running the last stretch together. Maybe her boyfriend is there to greet her. He's probably friends with him.* Will and this vision of athleticism, grace, and beauty crossed the finish line. He grabbed two bottles of water from the ice bucket. Handed her one first. They talked for a minute. She bent over laughing at something he said, and then they just casually disappeared into the crowd. Together. I was physically sick. My hands were shaking. I fumbled for my phone and texted Gracie, "Hey ... I hate to do this to you. I'm here. But I'm not feeling well all of a sudden. I'm headed home."

My Gram also used to say, "When you grow out of your kiddy britches, you can't try to crawl back in 'em. No matter what you do. They just won't fit."

***

Beauty and the Beast

After I made it through the crowd and the traffic— and into my driveway, the finality set in. I knew there was no going back. *It's life after Will.* A new chapter. But I also realized I still had to go back to the office. And if it wasn't awkward before, it surely would be now. I thought, *Maybe I should just tell Mr. Marley I'm done. No. I'll just tell Betty to tell Mr. Marley I'm done. Maybe tell Tammy to tell Betty. Ugh. Ridiculous. I'll do a professional email, thanking them for the opportunity.* I typed one out on my laptop in bed. Mostly lies.

I'm so grateful for this opportunity. Blah, blah. I so enjoyed working with all of you. I learned so much. Invaluable experience. Delete. Delete. Blah, blah. All the Best, No. Regretfully. Delete, delete. Sincerely ... Blah, blah, blah.

But instead of hitting send, I saved it to drafts and went to bed.

It was the first year I had ever missed fireworks. I could hear them faintly from my house. As I lay there in the bed that I made for myself, literally and figuratively, I imagined them sitting on the grass in front of the courthouse. *She's probably snuggled up to his side and looking up with her head on his shoulder. He's falling in love with how her long, soft brown hair smells and feels against him. I bet she's uncomplicated. Compliant. Not a Jezebel bone in her body. She'll make perfect potatoes* au gratin *and a big fuss over him. Always encouraging with his golf game. His biggest fan. Always making sure the whole world revolves around him. Day and night. Until death do they part.*

Gus crawled up on my chest and just stared at me. He didn't do his usual purring or nudging for me to scratch his head. It was like he knew. I wasn't really crying. Ugly crying anyway. But as I lay there, tears freely flowed down my face like they had been waiting lifetimes to be released. A bittersweet release. The complete release of a life that was never really mine.

The truth will set you free if it doesn't kill you first. I don't remember who said that either.

I went into the office the next day. Driving in, it occurred to me there may have been more to the sudden shift in how I was treated. Will was the golden child. He had grown up in that office. Their loyalty was clearly to him. *Maybe Betty knew that her "Ginger Baby" had his eye on her these last few weeks. Maybe his dad knew but also knew we had to get through the rest of this "employment agreement" without any unnecessary drama. Bad for public relations. Maybe they all knew her. Maybe she was a family member of someone there. Maybe they were rooting for her and just waiting on me to go back to school and get out of the picture.* All I knew for sure was I couldn't stay. None of it mattered now. I would quietly bow out. Swallow my pride. *I'll send the email tonight. In the meantime, going in for one last day will give me a chance to get my things out of my desk.*

That day, Betty needed an errand run. *This would burn some of my afternoon.* There were several large boxes to be delivered. I had to take the Suburban. It was big, awkward, and outdated just like the cheapskate funeral director's office. I hated driving the Suburban. A Suburban should require special training. A whole different license. At least a course. I mean ... there's like a whole additional vehicle to consider on the back end.

So, on the day I should have just sent the email and stayed in bed, right there in front of Bentley's Dry Cleaners, I got into the turning lane and heard the most horrendous noise. *Dammit.* I had sideswiped the front of another car. I got out. It was not just another car. It was what looked like a brand-new Jaguar. Temporary tags. The driver got out. He cursed me under his breath. Called 911. He barked, "Don't leave." *Like I would leave. I mean, I can't drive a Suburban. That doesn't mean I'm some kind of criminal.* He got back in his car. He was yelling at someone on his phone. I imagined he was taking it out on someone else—"kicking the dog"—so to speak. I didn't know what to do. I just knew I should have sent that email. I could have been somewhere completely different. And he could have been on his way to wherever people with brand-new Jaguars go at two o'clock in the afternoon. I started to call the office and changed my mind. By that time, the police were there. They did the report.

I drove slowly back to the office. I tried to park in its space out front, and Mr. Marley charged out of the front door. I guessed that someone from the office had seen me sitting in the turning lane sometime during the whole incident, and the news had beaten me there. He was angry. No doubt. He motioned me to park around back.

My heart was racing. I slowly pulled down the side street and in front of the back doors. *I guess this is where he means. I don't know.* Suddenly, Mr. Marley, Jim, and some other man I had never seen in my life stormed out of the back door. I got out. They paid no attention to me. *They will rely on the report, I guess.* They circled the vehicle multiple times. Inspecting every square inch. Then, they casually talked about the tread on the tires. I thought, *what in the hell?* Not one of them asked how I was. Was I hurt? Am I shaken up? Nothing. They just talked amongst themselves. Mr. Marley finally walked over to me and put his hand out for the keys. He looked at my hair. No expression. Back at me. Not a word.

And as he was walking off, I heard him say, "She was my wife's bright idea."

The guy that I didn't know said, "Well, somebody needs to teach her how to drive." They all laughed.

Mr. Marley stopped, slowly examined the keys like he was making sure that they were all still there, and replied in a more serious tone, "Somebody needs to teach her how to keep her mouth shut. That's what somebody needs to teach her. She thinks she's some kind of Joan of Arc. She's just a little freak. I have no idea what my son ever saw in her. Or my wife. Just her latest charity case, I guess."

Jim and the other guy chuckled. Mr. Marley finally put the keys in his pocket as Jim opened the door for him.

I really had nothing to lose now. There was no "good reference" to be had. *He's going to think Joan of Arc. He's going to see a freak. A charity case.*

Jezebel had been summoned. As was the spirit of every female that had been ignored, mistreated, used, or forgotten by the Bill Marleys of the world.

I said ... "Ummmm ... could you repeat that, Bill?"

He turned around. The guys' faces suddenly got serious. Jim let go of the door. Mr. Marley said, "What?" Sarcastically. Like he was bothered by my existence.

"You heard me, Bill. You said it was your wife's bright idea ... something about Joan of Arc ... and let's see ... somebody being a freak. A charity case?"

He kind of did this motion with his hand, almost shooing me away and said, "You're free to go, Laine. Please. Just go."

I said, "Well, that's good because I was already leaving, and I'll never be back. And you know what, Bill? You see, Bill—I'll leave—and you will forever be chained to your almighty money and your big fat ego, Bill. And your outdated ideas. And you will rot in that God awful funeral home of an office with those ridiculous fake columns and dusty fake plants thinking you are superior to me and everyone else. But you will be wrong, Bill. You are a big fish in a little bitty cesspool of a bowl, Bill. And you know that wife with the 'bright idea' of hiring me? You don't deserve her. She has more character and brains in the end of her little pinkie finger than you have in your entire body ... Bill. And Jim ... as for you, you are nothing more than an ass-kissing little coward. That's right. I said it. An ass-kissing coward." Jim's eyes dropped. I felt a pang of guilt for that one. But not for anything I said to "Bill." That was for all of us Jezebels.

Then, I realized I had forgotten my purse. *Dammit to hell.* I opened the door of the Suburban—got it—turned to look at them all just standing there speechless. I slammed the door as hard as I could and said, "By the way, Bill ... your precious Suburban smells like armpits. It's ready for the junkyard anyway."

I don't even remember walking back in the building. I was shaking. *I just need my things. Straight in and straight out.* Tammy looked at me almost with a smirk—like she was the lucky one—still on the *inside*. Still in "Mr. Marley's good graces." Tammy will spend the rest of her life keeping the *front*, like she said, "presentable."

Chapter 3

Him/Her

I finally made it back to campus with my car loaded down. It was bustling with people. Happy people. Tan and fresh from their summer vacations. Just like last year, there was excitement in the air. But unlike last year, I came alone. My parents had given me an obligatory send-off in the driveway. With the loss of my "lottery ticket," my beautiful "mane"—and my reputation after the "kind of" firing from the Marley's firm, I felt like I was worth much less to them now. They were beyond disappointed. And sometimes disappointment feels worse than anger.

But I was glad to be back—for lots of reasons. A university is a unique thing if you think about it. Unlike anywhere else, its whole existence is for the purpose of learning and growing ideas. Unlike high school, the learning was not just about someone else's ideas or conclusions being passed down, regurgitated. At a research university, anyway, people are coming up with new ideas and coming to new conclusions. Some that had possibly never even been considered. Especially in the school of science, the story was never over.

Of course, it may take years for their new ideas to make it to the mainstream. And don't get me wrong, science can be as bad as religion in some ways. If an old crusty dinosaur of a professor passionately teaches one theory for enough years, it's kind of like having to admit they are wrong when something new is discovered that debunks it. Think about it. Like your whole career was a big fat mistake. If you had written textbooks, you can't even sell them anymore. Some can never accept it. But for the most part, science is forward moving. As quickly as this universe is expanding, we are expanding our minds right along with it, as well as our capacity to understand it. In research, questions are welcomed. Encouraged. Necessary.

The campus felt like a big sigh of relief for my soul. A pretty safe place for an ocean dweller.

And this year was kind of a fresh start in lots of ways. I had a different room. And I had randomly been given a new roommate. Flora. When I finally made it back to my dorm, I nervously found my keycard. She wasn't in the room. But her things were, and she was already unpacked. I unpacked a few of my own things and made my bed. I decided against some of my decorations from last year. It's not like the first year having a dorm room. I didn't need cute. I needed a clean bed and a place to shower. And her things were mostly practical. Simple. A few photos. Her cat in a lobster Halloween costume. Good start. She's a cat person. A picture of a guy holding up a starfish on a beach somewhere. He looks pretty normal. I got my things mostly unpacked. Stopped to have some cantaloupe that I had picked up at the student center and scrolled through my phone.

But soon, my curiosity got the best of me. I walked over to her closet. I nervously opened it. *Okay ... hmmmm. Well, they are going to love this back home. I cut all my hair off, and now I'm living with a cross-dresser. Maybe transitioning. I'm not sure.* I went back over to look at the picture. *She/He. Is that him/her ... them. It looks like a guy. Her/his closet is basically a thrift shop of old men's clothing. Brown and grey men's suits, hats, a couple of ties. Lots of high tops. Every color. That's pretty cool, I guess. But the suits. I mean ... really? Suits? Who wears suits to class? And I'm talking like Grandpa clothes. A transitioning Grandpa. Ugh. I so don't need this right now. No hate, but why can't I just have a normal roommate?* Then, suddenly, I found the humor in it all. I laughed out loud and said, "I need to speak to a manager, please."

On cue, there was a banging on the door. I laughed again. "Now, that's service." I peeked out the eyehole. It was a guy ... *maybe him/her. I don't know.* But they looked legitimate, and the hall was full of people. So, I opened it. There was the person in the picture. I was sure of it. Very male looking. A box full of books on the ground. He/she said, "Are you Laine?" I replied, "Are you Flora?" We both laughed nervously. Then, around the corner came a tall and lanky girl in baggy rolled up khakis, a ratty concert T-shirt and yellow high tops. She yelled, "Hey, hey, hey ... my new roomie!" Before I could answer, she said, "This is James—my guy." As I was processing all of it, they made their way through the door with the box of books. Flora was most definitely a she.

James asked if I wanted to grab food with them. He said, "We are thinking tacos." I replied, "Ummm. Did you say food?" I cleaned up my cantaloupe, got my bag, and followed them downstairs. A couple of people spoke to Flora on the way down. She seemed likable. Safe. Familiar somehow.

***

Cathedral

That week, we got all of the kinks worked out in our schedules and found our classes. I had no idea how much learning I had to do that year—in and out of the classroom. I knew my classes were going to be tough that semester. I had a little bit of money in savings. I had my meal card and gas money. I decided to wait until after Christmas break to work. Flora was there on a full ride but had to work a few hours a week on campus. James wasn't working. We were all pretty serious students. So, Flora and James became my little family. I was careful to give them enough space. But strangely, I never felt like a third wheel.

I had a spot on the eighth floor of the library that became my second home. I loved it there. It was quiet. The view was incredible. In the clouds, perched right up there with the billions of carefully selected words of all of these thinkers, seekers, deep divers. Ocean dwellers. The library was my Cathedral. I wasn't thinking a lot about "church" or even God those days, but I actually had a kind of spiritual experience up there one Sunday afternoon.

It just happened out of the blue. And I only remember it was Sunday because the library was almost empty and the study rooms were closed. I had a book open and had been highlighting my notes. I was studying for a test. I stopped for a second. A beam of sunlight was shining through the window. I closed my eyes and just sat in its warmth. And suddenly, my whole body felt like—like it was smiling—every cell. And I know this is going to sound strange, but it was like my body just disappeared. My physical body. It was like I was just pure energy. And when I opened my eyes to get some sense of reality, on the ledge of the building was a tiny sparrow looking right at me. Inches away. It seemed to cock its head to study me. Ancient and brand new at the same time. A whole universe in every strand of every feather. God's DNA imprinted on each tiny one. That's when—I believe—maybe for the first time in my life, I felt God. Not the God that burns people in hell. The God that pulses through every living thing in this universe. Every atom. It was like for one brief moment, my heart synced with its collective heartbeat. I wasn't looking for this experience. I definitely didn't deserve it. Yet, there I was—the freak, the Joan of Arc, the charity case, the Jezebel—fully embraced by this Divine Love on a random Sunday afternoon on the eighth floor of a library— eleven hours from home.

And this is where my own God story took a turn.
Gabe said that Spirit knows when you are ready.
I haven't introduced you to Gabe yet.
I promise. I'm getting there.

***

He's the Man

As stressful as my days had become with class, labs, endless papers to write, my evenings were equally blissful. Flora was a balm to my bruised soul. She was funny. And we both loved to talk about mind-bending things. Nothing was too *woo-woo*. There was this complete freedom to be myself. I had never known that—even with my closest friends at home. With them, there were always limits. I knew where the line was drawn. My talks with Flora usually revolved around a controversial news story or something I had learned in my classes. She didn't love science like I did. She was a numbers person. Logical thinker. But she was always up for the pondering and the wondering. No idea was too deep or outlandish. Just a couple of ocean dwellers swimming happily together in the depths.

James joined us sometimes. Before we started cooking, he would bring us delicious food from a Thai place near campus. James' passion was anything to do with the brain. His sights were on medical school. He came from a long line of physicians. His father was an anesthesiologist. His sister was already in med school in Texas. James wanted to specialize in behavior. The physiological and chemical reasons we do some of the things we do. This always brought a welcome twist to our talks. He was funny too. And when they both got going, it was like watching a well-rehearsed dance. One just fueled the other's ideas and ridiculousness. It kind of made me miss Will sometimes. Will in the beginning anyway. James and Flora had been together for just short of two years. How could he still be so eager to make her laugh, listen to her so intently, pursue her? He already had her. That was quite obvious. Maybe it was because she let him pursue her. And she offered up the same attention when he talked about something important to him. Either way, they both knew their part in this dance and performed it seamlessly.

But I have to admit in my shallowness, I wondered about how much better it could be if Flora dolled up once in a bit. I mean ... Flora is beautiful. Her skin is fair and quite literally perfect. She is just shy of six feet tall. Her features are like art. Unusual. Striking. She easily could have modeled if she wanted. I could never imagine Flora in a dress or anything like that. The thought of it was almost comical. Yet, I still wondered if James wished she dressed more feminine. Like ... a girl, I guess. I soon realized, she may have been the most feminine 'she' I had ever met. Her clothes just didn't announce it. And James was in love with her soul—not her wardrobe.

James and Flora were "good people" as my dad would say. But different from my dad's version of "good people." Dad's version kept the yard of their brick rancher impeccably groomed, paid cash for their cars, held steady and respectable jobs, and never caused any trouble in their community. Those were the main qualifications anyway. James and Flora were a different kind of "good."

One thing I learned pretty quickly was that neither of them found pleasure in complaining or criticizing. Not like I did. I loved it. If someone in my class ticked me off, and I came back to the room wanting to rant, I was met with this almost uncomfortable resistance to it. I mean, Flora would listen. She was never dismissive or rude, but about forty-five seconds in, I would feel almost embarrassed to have even brought it up. My anger usually just dissipated and we would move on to more important topics—like what's for dinner. I realized she was giving them the same grace she offered to me. I didn't love that at first. I wanted to roll around in my misery—state my case of how this person or that person had been in the wrong—at least for a few minutes. She had zero interest in that. Flora's passion was good food. She loved to cook and started whipping us up some interesting dishes in the kitchen on our hall.

This is when I learned that healthy food and unconditional love are two of the most healing forces on the planet. And I had large doses of them both.

If Flora cooked and James was going to be there, we would take it down to one of the "Gathering Places" on the first floor of the dorm. James would always say, "Shall we gather this evening?" Flora would always respond, "Let us gather, my love" in some kind of medieval accent. We would all laugh. And there I was, their only child. More like their *student.*

One night, we were eating kind of late. Flora would obsess over one vegetable at a time. Experimenting with it for weeks before moving on to another. I would look up the nutritional value of each vegetable on my phone. I would do the commentary about it as she would meticulously do the prep. Pretending we had a cooking show and an audience hanging on our every word. Her newest obsession was eggplant. James joined us. We were eating and talking as usual. Flora had on her little "Benjamin Franklin glasses"—as I called them. Sweater vest and tie. Her sleeves rolled up from laboring in the kitchen.

We pretty much had the room to ourselves when a pretty large group straggled in—maybe seven or eight guys. They had come for the game on the largest TV screen in the building and were very obviously drunk. The whole energy shifted in the room. They were loud. I immediately felt uneasy. James and Flora got quiet. We began hurrying to finish and clean up when one of the guys started staring at us. He nudged his friend. His friend turned around. They were looking straight at Flora. *Do they know her?* I was trying to assess what was happening.

James quickly ate his last bite and wiped his hands and mouth like he was preparing to get up. I was actually scared at this point. I thought, *Maybe there's history between them. It doesn't feel like their first encounter.* Then, the guy said, "There *IT* is." They both began laughing openly and obnoxiously. The whole group of guys was soon staring at Flora. She looked at me. The look of sadness in her eyes absolutely destroyed me. I felt that old familiar rage. Hot rage, like the rage I had when I wrecked the Suburban and told Bill Marley off.

I stood up like I was going to do something about it. My face was on fire. I looked at James. I said something like, "Oh, he's going to think IT!" I did this big fake laugh. I got up and started walking toward the guys. I don't know what I thought I was going to actually do when I got there. But James firmly said, "Laine, please no." I turned around, and he had this look in his eyes. It wasn't fear. Yes. He was getting ready for a fight. But not a physical one. Truly. James could have probably killed this guy with his bare hands. He had studied martial arts since he was a kid. James was lean and naturally strong. *And* sober. This guy was a sloppy drunk. James first turned all of his attention to Flora. He gently grabbed her hand. I was kind of frustrated with

James, but I wouldn't dare cause even more stress for Flora.

We finished cleaning up. James had brought dessert as he usually did. That night it was an assortment of cookies from a popular bakery off campus. When we were leaving, he walked confidently over to the guy and handed him the small brown bag of cookies. He looked the guy right in the eye and said something like "Here. We had these left. You guys are welcome to them. Have a good night" but not with one ounce of sarcasm. I snuck the guy the dirtiest look I could make. He looked back at me, ashamed.

James was clearly the victor of the battle. The stronger opponent. We all knew it. The guy's friend knew it too and physically distanced himself from him—like he was embarrassed to have even been a part of it. James walked back over to Flora. He put his arm around her and gently kissed her on her forehead. We didn't say a word walking back up the stairs. James was "the man" as they say. A spiritual badass in my book.

Gram asked that we have the Beatitudes on her funeral pamphlet when she died. They were also on a wall hanging in her kitchen. Blessed are the peacemakers. Blessed are the meek. Blessed are the merciful. I had just witnessed them in real time. I had never known a guy like James.

James rarely spoke about his formal religious teachings. *His* God story. I still don't know if he "deconstructed" any of his beliefs. I do know that his family is for the most part Jewish. I'm not going to pretend like I know a lot about the faith. I don't. But I do believe, for some people of the Jewish faith, their view of the afterlife is different. I believe there is more of an expectation that we do good deeds—but not for the fear of hell. His goodness didn't come from fear. That's all I knew for sure. James was a peacemaker for the sake of peace.

"Be wise as a serpent and gentle as a dove."
Jesus said that.

As we were washing our dishes in the kitchen that night I said, "From now on, you are Saint James."

James replied, "Wasn't he beheaded or something?"

I said, "I think that was John the Baptist. Maybe not. Either way, you are Saint James of West Hall from this day forward." I knighted him with a spatula.

He snapped the dish towel at me and said, "Okay ... Joan of Arc." I had forgotten I had told him about my little episode with Bill Marley. He said, "She was burned at the stake, ya know."

"It's no easy life being a revolutionary, I guess."

"No long life either apparently," James added.

Flora announced that the next vegetable would be the potato if we all lived long enough to see it.

***

Moonstruck

Flora and I did talk about our religious teachings one night. We found out we had more in common than we thought. For one, we both had church trauma, but hers was on a whole other level than my own. Flora was "unchurched" (as they say in the South), and her friend from school insisted she begin going with her to a Wednesday night group for kids their age. The girl's dad would drop them off. They got a meal and a lesson. Then, they got to play basketball or do a craft. She said she loved it at first. *Until*—the too familiar story—one of the college-aged youth leaders took notice of her.

She was around twelve years old. He made her super uncomfortable. She tried to avoid him at all costs. Then, that year at Halloween, instead of a haunted house, they had a "Resurrection Room." It was basically rooms in the basement of the church decorated to represent different "sins." A bloody drunk-driving crash scene room. A nightclub room. An overdose room. The goal was by the last room, decorated like "heaven," the kids would be so terrified and shaken up that they would get saved right there—ask Jesus into their hearts. Flora said they had adults ready to pray at the tables decorated like puffy, white clouds.

Anyway, as Flora made her way through the dark rooms, she lost her friend. She was alone and genuinely scared but not of the decorations. Not of the horrific scenes of fake blood and gore. She kept seeing the guy. The youth leader. He was tracking her, and when she was in the back hallway making her way through the arrows drawn to the next room, he pulled her into the janitor's closet. She didn't elaborate from there. I think the whole thing was pretty quick. But she was shaken to the core. She went home and cried herself to sleep in her mother's bed. She said her mother went to the church in her best dress and heels that Sunday morning. She sat through the service quietly—even the visitor's welcome—smiling and shaking hands with everyone around her. And when there was an altar call, she went to the mic at the front of the church and asked that this young man come to the front to confess the sin of "robbing her daughter of her innocence."

Flora was not there, but she said her friend told her that the whole congregation broke out into chaos. The organist stopped playing. Flora's mom glared at the guy who was sitting on the second pew. I guess she had scoped him out during the service. She stood waiting like she fully expected him to come up there. The minister finally took the mic from her and tried to recover from it as best as he could. The guy ran out the back doors.

Flora even seemed to offer him grace when talking about it. How she could was beyond me. Maybe she knew in setting him free, she would also be free. I hadn't learned that lesson yet. I would. But Flora's mom—oh, she was the Queen Jezebel. I do think that her mom publicly fighting for her helped Flora avoid some of the shame and trauma later. There was not a trace of it in her voice as she told me the story.

I once read that pain must be heard, held and believed to be released. Flora's mom not only held her pain, she went to war for it.

But Flora and I had something else in common. As extreme and imbalanced as my denomination could be about their beliefs, her mom could be equally as extreme. Her mom did all of these strange ceremonies with fire and practically worshiped the moon. Flora said if there was a full moon out, she would have all these things "charging" in the moonlight on the back patio of their apartment—her crystals, her singing bowls, her plants. Flora said she would even put her box of pads and tampons in the light to charge sometimes. I died laughing. But it was their normal. Her mom also loved science. She studied energy healing. Science is validating that. She was ahead of her time in some ways. But everything was to the extreme. Even so, I could tell that Flora loved that her mom was quirky. I felt like she was even proud of her for it. She raised Flora on her own.

And Flora understood all too well that it takes a lot of courage to be different. The kind of courage it takes to walk to the front of a large church on a crowded Sunday morning in your high heels and demand that your daughter's abuser repent on the spot.

Flora said the more practical problem was that she would also get obsessed with a guru every couple of years, spending all of their money to go listen to them speak all over the country. She would even borrow money to make the trips. She would put each new "savior" up on some type of pedestal while putting them in financial jeopardy doing so. She relied on charts and psychics for her every move. She had one that she would call regularly—$19.99 to find out if she should get on a plane, go to the doctor, buy a new car. Her mom had grown up in a strict Catholic home where you had to go through the priest to reach God. She definitely deconstructed her God story. Flora said she rebelled against it with all she had, but even as a kid, Flora had the insight to see that her mom was still putting other human beings in charge of her truth. It might as well have been a Catholic priest.

***

The Last Supper

Before I knew it, we were studying for finals. We didn't see much of each other during those couple of weeks. I was camped out on the eighth floor of the library, and our gatherings were replaced by a quick bite alone in the student center. We all were shooting for 4.0's. It was sleep, eat, class, study—and repeat. Finally, James and Flora were both done with their classes, and I had one final left. But it was one of my easiest and could be taken online. Flora suggested "we gather" for dinner before heading home for Christmas break. We decided to go all out.

When we had last gathered, it was still the potato. I had no idea the things that you could do with a humble potato. One night, she made these potato pancakes. A recipe that came from her German grandmother, Alma. Then she made some crispy potato fries. Seasoned perfectly. Garlic mashed potatoes, of course. I was excited to see what she would come up with next.

I volunteered to make a roast. I was no chef. But I remembered there was a slow cooker in the kitchen on our hall. I made sure it still worked, and I went to the Nature's Market for the best I could find—grass fed, "humanely raised," whatever that means. I also splurged on fresh garlic, rosemary, basil, and parsley.

It was Thursday night before we were all to leave for break. My roast had been cooking in the slow cooker all day with the fresh garlic and herbs. The aroma filled the hall. I kept sneaking in to check it as I studied for my last final. James said he was baking something in the oven in his dorm kitchen. A few hours before my roast was done, Flora came in from the store with a brown bag of her ingredients. She whipped it up as I took my last final online and showered. It would be our "last supper" before break. We said it jokingly, but it was quite literally—in that gathering place anyway.

We sat at the table closest to the fake Christmas tree adorned with white lights. I plugged it in and noticed a whole string missing near a few paper angels with Christmas wish lists on them. A sorority on campus was doing gifts for kids at a local club. Three were left hanging there. Forgotten.

I wondered if those three kids would just go without this year. Everybody in their class is getting something from Santa—except them. I grew up an only child, upper middle class. I'm sure my parents struggled just to come up with things to buy for me. My parents definitely didn't spoil me. My dad worked very hard to teach me the value of a dollar. But I got most of what I wanted all year long. I thought, *This has got to be pretty psychologically damaging to a kid. Poor. Probably rejected by peers. Their family is rejected by society, most likely. Then, here they are on December 25th and they get rejected by Jolly Saint Nick of all people. They have to wonder what they did wrong.*

Flora and I situated the roast on cheap dinnerware from the kitchen. Her surprise potato dish covered in foil. Our pre-made salad still in the clear bag. And we had three paper cups of red wine. That was risky. Against campus rules. Soon, James joined us with chocolate chip cookies and dinner rolls. We all grabbed a warm roll and swigged the last of our wine. A communion of sorts. Flora said a quick Native American prayer thanking the animal that had been sacrificed for our meal. She said it was something her mother always did. It felt right somehow.

Then Flora said, "You guys ready for the vegetable extraordinaire?" James said in a monotone voice, "Oh, what were we on now ... oh yeah ... the potato ... *again.*" I remind them of the nutritional value of the potato. I read aloud from my phone, "The potato is an excellent source of vitamin C ... and contains potassium ... and even quercetin. And quercetin has anti-cancer and cardio-protective qualities." We all burst out laughing. Maybe a little buzzed on our red wine—definitely happy to be together again and that the semester was over. Flora dramatically pulled the foil off the casserole dish. "Tada! Vegan potatoes *au gratin!*" I just about fell out of my chair laughing. They were confused. When I recovered,

I explained to them how there was almost a running contest between the ladies in my church back home of who could make the best potatoes *au gratin* at the covered dish dinners. Never a "vegan" one though. I couldn't imagine how that might go over with a bunch of die-hard Southern cooks.

And I guess that is what started the conversation about what it was like growing up in my church. Flora and I had talked about our church experiences that night in the room. I didn't really tell her much about mine after she shared her story. Mine seemed so insignificant in comparison. I was just going to kind of hit the high points with them. I didn't think about it much those days at school. My mind was too busy with Organic Chemistry and Microbiology.

But as I started talking ... and remembering ... there she was again. Jezebel. She must have been hibernating just beneath the surface. And she pretty much hijacked the dinner. James and Flora hadn't seen this side of me. I mean ... they knew I could be feisty. They definitely had seen that. But they hadn't witnessed my ugly bitterness. And the more I talked, the more I remembered. And the more I remembered, the more bitter I felt. And I couldn't stop remembering.

One experience led to the next. As I mentioned, neither of them found pleasure in attacking people— even large groups of people. Countries, institutions, religions ... or my church. People were people to them. All deserving of some grace. But they were wise enough to know that this needed to happen. Right then and there. Even if they couldn't understand it, they knew this pain came from my soul. And it was real and ran deep. I was soon crashing our dinner just like I had crashed Jesus' birthday party in the eighth grade. But nobody rolled their eyes or tried to shut me up this time. In fact, Flora stopped eating and came around the table. She leaned down and wrapped her arms around me as I let out long overdue sobs. James dropped his head. He may have been praying to his version of God. I don't really know. But years of frustration and rejection just poured out of me. I was safe with them. I was loved. Even in my bitterness, I was loved. I thought about Mrs. McCracken and my Valentine. Like her, they could see my light right through the mess of me. Somehow.

Suddenly, the doors opened. It was the janitor starting his deep cleaning list for break. He was struggling to get this big, yellow cart through the door. But when he looked up, he had this look on his face like he had accidentally walked into a delivery room. A birth. He gently shut the doors and tiptoed out, apologizing as he went. We all burst out laughing. I wiped the tears from my eyes. Maybe he had actually walked into a birth. A rebirth. Just one of several that I would have on that campus. On the way out, James, without saying a word, pulled the three angels off the tree and put them in his jacket pocket. And as he did, the string of missing lights flickered on again.

Chapter 4

Love Language

That semester, my mom's contact had been minimal at best. In her eyes, I was just having one of "my fits." Just rebelling. First, wrecking things with Will ... then "acting a fool" at Mr. Marley's office. Her words. She couldn't spank me so she would just passively punish me long distance with her silence. Isn't it funny how no matter how old you get, your parents think you are twelve? Like eternally stuck at twelve years old. Just in need of a good spanking. I'll do it to my kids too, I guess. It seems to be universal.

My dad had always been more logical about things and the driver in my education. He was invested in it, in more ways than one. Like I said, that was his father's alma mater. He lost him in an accident right before I was born. Me being there meant keeping him alive in some way. That school was insanely expensive. His bonus every year had gone toward my college fund. He was disappointed in me, but he continued doing dad things.

He would call me every Friday like clockwork. "You okay? How are your grades? How's your car running? Okay, your mother says 'hello.' We love you." Then, he would let me talk to Gus before hanging up.

Those calls were more important to me than I was willing to admit. And they eventually helped save my life.

I set out for the drive home for Christmas. I love driving. I guess it's that love of freedom. I stocked my car with good snacks. Mozzarella wrapped in prosciutto, edamame with sea salt, baby carrots, orange slices, chocolate covered almonds, two large bottles of sparkling water. And I downloaded some interesting podcasts. And, of course, my favorite new music.

First, I listened to a podcast about relationships. The guest was an "expert" in soul connections. I don't know how you become that exactly—"an expert" in matters of the soul. But it was all about "soulmates and twin flames." Anyway, she had just written a book. The host was a fan and a believer. Some of it I bought. Some, not so much. But she did say a few things that stuck with me. One was that she said we have many potential soulmates in our lifetime. And that we would gravitate to the ones we most resonated with—dependent on our own spiritual growth. That made good sense. I thought about James and Flora. They definitely resonated. I thought about Will. In the beginning, it felt like a soulmate kind of thing. But as I grew, I grew right out of him. *Maybe if*

I hadn't "grown," we could have been soulmates. Or maybe he actually grew out of me. I don't know.

I met Mom at the front door. As I was fumbling around for my house key, she opened it. She was in her robe. With just the glass door between us, she stopped and looked at me in the glow of the porch light. I saw my reflection in the glass. I had been so in my head the last few months, I realized I had definitely let myself go. I had on leggings and a long flannel shirt. My haircut had grown out some. That night, like most, I had it pulled back in a headband, pieces sticking out everywhere. No makeup. Thick wool socks with slides. I looked homeless. I felt homeless. She looked at me, not with disappointment this time, but with pity and maybe some remorse. She opened the door and gave me the biggest hug I could remember getting under that roof. In that random moment on our front porch, it felt like she completely let go of the vision of who she thought I *should* be and just accepted me for who I was—no strings attached.

Meanwhile, my dad went to the car, brought all my things in, checked the tires, and gave the car a good look under the security lights, like a dad does. Then, he came back in and looked at me—right past the mess of me— and said, "I missed you, Laine." He had such sadness in his eyes. It seemed like he was the child in that moment. *Was he tearing up?* The only times that I ever saw my dad cry were the rare times that he would talk about his dad. We weren't a mushy family. "Words of affirmation" definitely wasn't our love language. *Did we even have a love language?* We just stood there in our awkwardness. So, he picked up Gus, handed him to me and snapped us both out of it, saying, "He has been so annoying. He's a 24/7 meow machine. Usually wants out around 3 a.m. You can get up with him tonight." He walked away like his eyes weren't full of tears. I was happy to *finally* be home.

I think I was there about three days when I heard the scream. I ran to the basement. My mom had been trying to reach some Christmas decorations on a stool and had fallen. I called my dad. We took her to the emergency room. Her arm was fractured in two places. We got her comfortable. Dad and I made a pact that we would just pick up the slack with the cooking and laundry. But it wasn't twenty-four hours until the church started calling.

I had never seen more food in my life. A legion of earthly angels. Two potatoes *au gratin* in the garage freezer. And the prayer cards started coming in. Every time I went to the mailbox, I found some words of encouragement. One lady brought a case of toilet paper. Dad got a kick out of that. But this was my church at its best. Community at its best. I thought about breaking down with James and Flora. I felt ridiculous. I felt like a traitor. I was overwhelmed by their care for my mom. I was humbled—for the time being anyway.

The week of Christmas, my mom's sister, Patricia, her husband Jeff, and two twin girls, Audria and Andrea, had been planning to come. Despite Mom's injury, we all agreed that they all still should. Although, I wasn't Jeff's biggest fan, and he wasn't mine. I used to use Facebook to air all my opinions. I know, hard to imagine that. Right? And I don't even remember what it was about, but a couple of years ago, Jeff got mad at something I had shared. He called me all kinds of names right there on my post. Then, when I went to tag them in a photo a few months later, I realized the whole family had blocked me—even Jeff's sister whom I had only met twice. Blocked. Anyway, this was the first time I had even thought about it since before I left for school. People get over things. We've all had our less than proud moments on social media. I couldn't wait to see the girls.

That night, I helped Mom get ready for bed. I took a long shower. I thought about Will. I was surprised at how little he had even crossed my mind that semester. But I guess being home with some free space in my brain, he crept back in somehow. After my shower, I got in bed and opened my laptop. I didn't remember my password for Facebook. I created a new one. I found Will's mom ... *Catherine Marley.*

I had a sinking feeling as I clicked on her name. I scrolled. And there he was—*my* Will. Recent picture. Maybe fall break. A mission trip. There were about twelve of them in the photo. And there she was by his side. In my spot. Living out my life. He looked good. His hair longer. Even messier than his usual. He looked like he had just come off a run or a hike. Glowing. Happy. She was the reason behind that smile now. And I wasn't even close to the same person I was then. I studied my old profile picture for a long time. *Who was she?* A stranger to me. I closed my laptop. My aunt and uncle would be there in the morning.

***

The Monster

Their flight got there around eleven o'clock. Dad and I met them at the airport. We took them to the car rental place. Per usual, Jeff got the biggest, newest, flashiest SUV he could find. He followed us home to our humble split-level. A cranberry-red monster now sat in our driveway. My Aunt Patricia ran to my mom. It was sweet. Sisters. They regressed when they were together. Patricia dramatically and gently hugged my mom, kissed her fractured arm and did some kind of weird high-pitched voice. It's so strange to think that my mom was actually a kid once. But I loved hearing their stories about growing up. I was named after her. Patricia Elaine. My Gram gave me the nickname, "Laine." Well, she called me "Lainey."

I tried to be a good older cousin to their girls. They had just turned seven. I reintroduced them to Gus. I reminded them where the snacks were in the pantry, the desserts from church in the garage fridge. How to use the new remote to find their favorite shows and movies. Between looking after my mom and the girls, I felt useful and content. All was well.

Aunt Patricia and Mom stayed up late talking and laughing every night. Dad and Uncle Jeff watched every sporting event they could find. The TV in the den had never seen so much action. A lot of news, and my uncle's commentary, of course. Between the girls' movies and their TV binges, I craved solitude. I would retreat to my room or occasionally find a reason to go out, taking the long way back home. Sometimes in silence. Sometimes listening to my podcasts and my music. I wanted to run down by the river, but the air was frigid, and I was afraid I would see Will.

Everybody finally got tired of the TV. We all decided to pile into Uncle Jeff's SUV and go to the mall. It was two days before Christmas. This sounded like a terrible idea. But they talked me into it. I had heard Mom and Patricia talk about what the twins were getting for

Christmas. Some of it had been delivered to our house and tucked away weeks ago. I expected this would be a mall Santa encounter for the girls, lunch, a good dose of Christmas anticipation. Nope.

About four meltdowns by the girls and two hundred dollars worth of junk later, we were piled back into the red monster and headed home. I was grateful for my fiscally conservative parents at that moment. They weren't stingy like Mr. Marley but always thoughtful about how the impact of having "too much" would be on me.

Jeff had become "successful" quickly in a small loan business. His version of successful, anyway. He had four or five stores by that time. My dad always said it was a borderline unethical business model. I thought about those three angels on the tree back in the Gathering Place. No doubt, James had taken care of them. The excess I just witnessed almost felt like child abuse. They were robbing these girls of knowing the value of money while pumping them full of this artificial replacement for *true* joy. The pleasure in the simple things. Working for things. Waiting on things. Enjoying the things you already have. How would they ever find their way back to it?

To top it off, at the four-way going out of the mall, a car in front of us had stopped to give money to a guy who appeared to be homeless. The woman was leaning out of her car and saying something to the man. My Uncle Jeff started honking his horn. "Goooo onnnn." We finally passed him, and Jeff said under his breath, "Get a job, dude." My cousin glared at the man—mouth still blue from her seven-dollar ICEE that she threw a fit for and got. She yelled out the back window, "Yeah ... get a job, dude." Her sister said, "Yeah ... loooosssser." They looked at each other and laughed. My uncle smiled proudly at them in the rearview. If he wasn't driving, he would have high-fived them both.

I remembered why I hated Uncle Jeff, and I hated Aunt Patricia in that moment too. She sat there in silence. I knew she was better than that. My Gram taught her better than that. Not only was she no peacemaker. She was an accomplice to the murder of their daughters' little souls.

***

Christmas Stories

The next day was Christmas Eve. I woke up to the smell of pancakes my Aunt Patricia had made. The girls were running around the house chasing Gus. I stretched and smiled. It felt like a special day—even if Jesus wasn't really born on December 25th. Like the kid in Sunday school said, "Who cares?" *It's almost*

Christmas. I felt it. It was thick in the air. My dad had his own little tradition on Christmas Eve. He would shoot guns or cut wood. It was something his dad did. Grandpa Anderson was a big hunter. My dad wasn't a hunter at all. But he would cut wood on his friend's farm. Other times, he would go to the shooting range. I went with him a few times. I heard him and Uncle Jeff talking downstairs. It sounded like a shooting range day this year. I couldn't imagine Jeff actually doing the hard labor of cutting wood—and it was so cold outside— spitting snow off and on all morning.

I finally heard them get into "the monster" and pull out of the driveway. I went to the kitchen. The girls were eating their pancakes. I picked up Gus. I said, "Girls day, Gussy!" The girls cheered. There is no such thing as a bad kid. There are traumatized kids. There are products-of-sloppy-parenting kids. There are repeating-what-they've-been-taught kids. There are kids with legitimate medical reasons for acting out. But no bad kids. Not one.

My mom informed me that my dad and Jeff planned to be back to watch the girls and she, Patricia, and I were going to the five o'clock silent communion at church. I was relieved. I knew there was no way I was getting out of going there at some point. The seven o'clock service was when they had the children's program. That's the one the Marleys would attend—and almost everyone else that I most certainly did not want to see. And the "silent" in silent communion worked for me. I wouldn't have to talk to anyone. After stuffing ourselves with pancakes, the girls and I watched some of the old Disney classics together. They snuggled right up to me. I imagined having two little girls of my own one day.

That afternoon, after helping Mom fix her hair, I dressed for the service. We all layered in heavy coats and scarves. I drove my car. Just pulling in the parking lot felt so strange. So many memories there. Good and bad. It really hadn't been that long since I had been there, but somehow, it felt like decades. We walked in. The building was warm. There was fresh greenery draped on the pews. All the candles were lit up front. I saw a few people I knew. They smiled. They gave special attention to my mom, who had her arm in a sling. There were only maybe thirty or forty people there. Many elderly. We quietly slid into the second row.

As I sat there, the familiar feeling of that wooden pew and the smell of the sanctuary overwhelmed me. Have you ever noticed that all churches have the same smell? You know the smell. Like freshly brewed coffee and old newspapers ... maybe mixed in with a baked casserole. The years of opening hymnals and covered dish dinners floating through the air, I guess. It's not unpleasant. And it was all so familiar. The organist gently played some Christmas music. The pastor and several men in the church uncovered the communion up front. It was draped in a white tablecloth. Grape juice in tiny mouthwash cups. Baskets full of cardboard-like wafers. I had been a part of it a million times. I knew the routine like the back of my hand. It had not changed one bit. But I had. I had no hatred for the pastor now. I felt no need to pick any fights. In that moment anyway, my wound felt healed—at least scabbed over.

Now, I would love to tell you I went home and washed everyone's feet with Frankincense and Myrrh before retiring to my bed to pray. But I'm no Jesus. Not even a James.

And Gabe—I promise I'm getting to Gabe—taught me that spiritual growth is not linear. He said that especially before you learn to master yourself—gentle your ego—there can be lots of highs and lows. I was about to experience both within hours of each other.

When we came home, the monster was back in the driveway and the news blaring in the den. Uncle Jeff was griping about the immigrants coming in. "Diseased, druggies ... just look at them." My dad was mostly neutral in these situations. If it didn't pertain directly to him or the economy, he barely cared. His neutrality seemed to frustrate Jeff that night. He got louder and louder. He went on to talk about "the rapists, the drug lords, the murderers," giving examples of how these "bums" were just destroying our country, our "Christian nation." He kept saying, "They are trying to kick God out of everything. That's what's wrong with this country. We kicked God out of it."

Now, I know there have to be laws. There has to be order. My Uncle Jeff was not wrong about that—not in the least. But he talked about these people like they weren't even human beings. And like *our* God wasn't *their* God too. Like God had drawn the lines between the countries on our planet. Separating us from these *animals.*

I thought about the immigrants who had built all the houses in Will's neighborhood. Million-dollar homes. The hot sun beating down on them. Never missing a day's work, arriving at the construction site piled into one small vehicle. Doing jobs that nobody else wanted to do. I thought about the immigrants I always saw in the fields when we drove to the beach for our summer vacations. On the way home, we always stopped at the farmers' market to load up on ripe tomatoes, cucumbers, and peaches they had grown. A few crinkled dollars exchanged for all their hard work. Their attempt at freedom and a good life for themselves and their own families. I thought about Maya, a student I graduated from high school with, who was one of the smartest girls in our class. I knew her family had probably not come to our country legally. But Maya had no other choice than to come with them. And she not only learned our language—she mastered it. She worked harder than any student in our class.

There may be murderers and drug dealers that come over the border. But there are also these people. Human beings trying to find safety and happiness. Also God's children. On a planet that He created for all of us.

I tuned Jeff out and went to help Patricia get the food ready in the dining room. The girls and I put on some jazzy Christmas music. They were dancing around with Gus. He was miserable. I remembered I had a little candy cane Christmas sweater for him. The girls helped me dig it out of the decorations box in the garage. We put it on him, and we danced around the living room. Finally, we all stuffed ourselves with hors d'oeuvres and Christmas cookies sent by the church. We were just enjoying the tree. Mom and Patricia were talking about Christmas at Gram's.

I think it was Mom who first heard the carolers in the distance. They didn't come every year. This was a special treat. I told the girls that they would stop by our door and sing for us. They both made a face like they thought the whole thing was odd. I guess it was if you had never experienced it—or even heard of it. I went to get my coat and helped them with theirs. My mom said something to Patricia about it being an all-men's choir from the Unitarian Church. Our neighbors were members. My Uncle Jeff got up from his chair and said,

"Well, I'm out. I'm not going to stand in the cold to hear a bunch of fags sing."

My whole body tightened up. I thought about James.

The rest of us layered up and went out on the porch. Dad stood in the doorway. Hands in his pockets. Mom said, "Here they come!" The girls jumped up and down as their voices got louder and closer. Finally, the singers were in front of our house. The singing stopped for a minute as they situated themselves in two rows. Then, the director motioned them. I stood there with a lump in my throat—literally fighting back tears as they sang the most beautiful *a cappella* rendition of "Oh Holy Night." We pulled our hands from our coat pockets and clapped as loudly as we could. The girls ran to them and hugged them, making their way to each one. I noticed that several of them were tearing up. One bent down to talk to them. He told them his name was Michael. They both hugged him again. I imagined that many of them endured a lifetime of rejection by their families on holidays. *Maybe some of them had no other place to be tonight.*

Patricia hurried the girls back into the warm house. Mom and I stood on the porch and listened to them break into another song as they walked to the Millers. She slid her good arm through mine. We vowed that we would carol the neighborhood with them next year and broke out into a terrible attempt at "Joy to the World."

Inside, Aunt Patricia helped the girls out of their coats. Mom and I came in and I said, "Who wants hot chocolate with marshmallows?" They cheered. More jumping up and down. Audria began doing splits and cartwheels in the living room. Finally, they settled on their stools, and I opened a bag of extra-large marshmallows.

Andrea said, "Laine, what does fag mean?" It was like a punch in the stomach even hearing that word come out of her mouth. I was disgusted. And sad.

As I carefully placed a marshmallow in each cup, I thought, *How do I even handle this without ripping their father to shreds?* "Well Andrea, it really just stands for something." They looked confused. I explained, "F is for Fearless, A is for And, G is for Gentle. Fearless and gentle. That's what it means. Fearless and gentle."

Audria said, "Oh! I love fags! They are nice!"

Andrea's eyes lit up. She said, "And they sing real good too!" They both began poking their marshmallows under the cocoa and giggling when they popped back up. I watched them and wondered who they would become.

It's terrifying isn't it, how malleable these little minds are. With enough persistence, you could teach them to hate anyone. Anyone. Suddenly, I felt a little of that old rage bubbling.

It came time for the Christmas story. It was our tradition every Christmas Eve. Since I was old enough to read, we took turns. I loved it when it was my turn as a kid. My mom said, "Hey, Laine, go grab my Bible out of my nightstand." I think she just assumed I would want to read it. Instead, I handed it to Uncle Jeff. I said, "Would you read it for us this year?" He took the Bible nervously. Every eye was on him. I knew pretty quickly he didn't know where to find the story in scripture. He had no clue. I could have easily helped him without anyone even noticing. That's what James would have done. I didn't. I sat there enjoying the whole struggle.

I know ... and fresh out of church even. Oh ... it gets worse. Much worse.

As everyone quieted down to hear him read, I said, "Jeff, before you open to the Christmas story, do you mind reading some other stories for us?"

He nervously said, "Sure ... I guess so ... which ones?"

"The ones where Jesus calls people fags. Those stories. Read those first. In fact, I want to hear about all of the stories where Jesus rails against 'the fags.'"

My mom closed her eyes. Jeff looked at me with sheer hatred. I didn't care by this point. It was too late to turn back.

I said, "And Jeff ... then, you can flip on over and read about the man and woman who were traveling and were forced to have their baby in the manger—you know Joseph and Mary. Ever heard of them? Those bums? Their bum child probably grew up just to destroy

Bethlehem. Probably became a diseased drug lord or something. I want to hear all about that too. Oh. And after that, flip on over to where Jesus says it's easier for a camel to go through the eye of a needle than a rich man to get into heaven. What do you think that means, Jeff? Any clue? I've always wondered. Do you think that big red SUV you've been bullying people in all week will fit through the eye of the needle, Jeff? Oh ... then ... turn on over to the story of the Good Samaritan. You know *that* story. The one where he tells the guy to get a job. I love that story. Read that one too."

Jeff tossed the Bible on the couch next to my mom. He looked at me and said, "Idiot. You think you are somebody now at your fancy college. Don't you? You don't know anything. And you are probably costing your daddy a hundred G's a year to be what, Laine? Let me guess ... a public school teacher. So, you can do what ... make forty a year brainwashing our children with your liberal bullshit? And I heard you indoctrinating my girls up there in the kitchen. You didn't think I heard you. Did you?" He clenched his jaw. "Did you? The Bible is clear about one thing. It says homosexuality is a sin. It's God's word. Maybe you need to read that part."

He got up and headed to the den. As he was walking down the stairs, I said, "Hey Jeff ... by the way, did I hear your sister just remarried? That's unfortunate for her. Her being an adulterer now and all. It says it right there in the New Testament that if a man divorces his wife for anything but sexual immorality and she remarries, he makes her an adulterer. God's word. And I saw you checking out all the women at the mall. Flirting with that cashier. She really liked you. Jesus said that if you even look at a woman with lust, you've already committed adultery. It's right there in the Bible. Book of Mathew. God's word. It's not far from that Christmas story you couldn't even find. And we don't even want to get into the Old Testament. I sure hope Patricia was a virgin when you married. If not…you know you can stone her to death. It's right there in Deuteronomy. And I sure hope you guys don't mix your flax with linen or eat shellfish or get tattoos or cut your hair or work on the Sabbath ... or pierce your ears. Leviticus. God's word. But never mind. You can't even find one of the most important stories in the whole book." Jeff was already downstairs and out of sight.

The girls looked at me. Andrea nervously fiddled with her new snowflake earrings. Only minutes ago, they were so excited to hear the story about baby Jesus. Now, they sat there on the hearth, looking at me with their new matching Christmas pajamas—with only a hollow sadness in their eyes. I was a hypocrite. We were all sorry hypocrites. My dad suggested we skip the story and all just go to bed. Mom already had.

Have you ever had an emotional hangover? It's a thing. Not one drop of alcohol, but you wake up feeling like you've had a whole bottle.

I rolled over the next morning to the sound of the girls tearing through their gifts. Kids are so resilient. For them, nothing had happened. I mean ... they will probably tell their own "Christmas stories" to a counselor one day when they are thirty-two. The one where their cousin and their dad brawled on Christmas Eve over some Bible verses. But not today. Today, they were unbothered by any of it. For me, I wanted to slither to my car, drive back to school, never to be heard from again. I lay there going over the night before. As the details came into focus, I thought, *Dear God ... I wish it were a dream.*

The girls busted through the door, "Get up, get up, get up!" Andrea had Gus in a tight squeeze. *It wasn't a dream.*

"I'll be there in a minute. And I want to see every present. I mean it!" I delayed getting out of bed as long as I could. Scrolling through my photos I had taken over the last few days, I found Gussy in his Christmas sweater. I sent it to my group text with James and Flora.

"Merry Christmas! Ohmygosh. I can't wait to get back and see you guys!"

James texted back, "Hope Santa was good to you."

Flora wrote, "He's so handsome in his little sweater. Merry Christmas, Laine :)"

I replied to her, "I'll put his picture next to Max's."

Flora didn't reply to me. I got a weird vibe. *I'm sure it's fine. It's Christmas morning. They are probably just crazy busy. I've just got a week, and I can get back there to my safe place. Safe from these people. More like safe from who I am when I am with them.*

On the drive back, I listened to more of the podcast on relationships. I thought, *Clearly I suck at all of them. Every one. Maybe there was another annoying soul that would "resonate" with me—that crashes family holidays and traumatizes little children on Christmas Eve. Ruiners. Mr. and Mrs. Ruiner. We could annoy each other and just ruin things until the end of time.*

Chapter 5

Hard Pill

I got back to the dorm late. After midnight. I kind of expected that Flora would have beaten me there. It was too late to text. The next morning, I took a long shower. I was putting some of my clothes back in my closet—some new sweaters Mom bought me. I felt this overwhelming sadness. I couldn't shake it. Like post-holiday blues but way worse. Bordering on hopelessness. I hated myself. And you know the old saying—you can't really run away from yourself—or trust me, I would have.

I got a text from James. "Hey Laine ... mind if I drop by for a second?"

"Sure. What's up?"

He just replied, "I'll meet you downstairs."

I looked over at Flora's things. I went straight to the front entrance. I finally saw James walking up the sidewalk. He came in and gave me a tight hug. Then, he led the way over to some couches. My stomach was feeling sick by this point. *Something is very wrong.*

"Laine ... Flora wanted me to tell you this in person." I thought, *Well, she asked him to come. At least she isn't dead. I bet they are broken up ... that's it. Oh my God. They broke up. How?*

He continued, "You know her mom has had a lot of health problems."

"Yeah, MS ... some other things ... right?"

"Yeah, she has several autoimmune conditions. But the MS has gotten much worse. Over Christmas, her mom went blind."

"Oh my God. Completely blind?"

"No," he said very calmly, like a future physician would. "Not permanently. She has gotten her vision back ... for the most part. They have her on a trial medication. She's very unstable right now. She's adjusting to the medication for one, but the stress of it all has really taken a toll on her."

"So, what does this mean for Flora? When will she be back?"

He dropped his shoulders and let out a long sigh. "I don't know, Laine. She doesn't know. Everything is so unpredictable. The disease is so unpredictable. And she is all that her mom has."

Suddenly, I wanted to make her mom out to be some kind of villain. "She can't expect her to just leave school. To just up and leave her life. To leave you—to leave us."

I looked over to the doors of the Gathering Place. I could almost hear the slam of that chapter closing. Last semester suddenly felt like a lifetime ago.

James had no words to comfort me. And I needed to get my thoughts together before calling Flora. I went back to the room. I felt this weird sinking feeling. Kind of like fear, but it consumed my whole body. It was physical. *Am I coming down with something?* I shook it off and forced myself to call her.

Flora told me the whole story herself, from start to finish. She seemed to have accepted the idea of not coming back. She had a lot more time to process it, I guess. I was looking for a glimmer of hope. I said, "Well, how is she eating? You know people have gone into complete remission from autoimmune with diet. Is she doing red meat? Sugar? Is she on Omega-3's? Please tell me she's not eating gluten. That's just fuel to the fire, Flora. I have this cleanse she needs to do, and then we just need to get her on the right diet. Are you cooking for her? She needs anti-inflammatory foods. Fresh. No leftovers. They can be moldy and cause a histamine reaction. Is she sensitive to histamines? That means she really needs to work on her gut health. Do you know? You need to find out, Flora. Oh. And no nightshade vegetables. Well, I know that's true for other autoimmune conditions. Probably hers too. I would just avoid them altogether. I have my juicer she can borrow.

She can just have it. Actually, I'll just order her a new one on Amazon. I'll have it delivered here, and you can get it when you visit—or come back." I was clearly desperate by this point.

She let me ramble on, and then there was a heavy silence. She said slowly, "Actually, Laine, James is bringing me my things next weekend. I can't leave Mom alone long enough for a visit."

I was kind of lightheaded. My heart was racing. Neither of us could find a positive note to end the conversation on. So, she just said, "Listen. I will call you soon. It's all going to be okay, Laine. I promise. It's all going to be fine." As I sat my phone on my nightstand, I thought, *Is it? Is it all going to be fine?* Suddenly, the campus felt dark. Foreign. I can't find a better word for it.

I managed to find my classes. I had to switch one around. It was a hassle. It kept my mind occupied. And that first week, I was living in denial. Her clothes and things were still there. Max's and James' pictures by her bed. Then after taking my laundry and going to the store on that Saturday, I came back to the room. Everything was gone. Everything. I had forgotten James told me he would come on Saturday. Or maybe I chose to forget.

I opened her closet, and the emptiness swallowed me whole. The pictures gone. Like she never existed. This felt more like a death than breaking up with Will did. And I didn't just lose her. I had lost James too. I felt like I had lost everyone. I looked at the sandwich I had brought back for dinner. I no longer wanted it. I no longer wanted to be here. I didn't want to be anywhere.

That night, James texted me, "Laine, I'm still around. Please don't be a stranger." Of course, I replied that I would stay in touch—knowing I probably wouldn't make the effort. Not anytime soon anyway. It took all I had in that moment just to respond to his text. I knew it was going to take everything I had in me to get through that semester.

Now, I consider myself to be a pretty resilient person. I have a few healthy coping skills. Those first few weeks, I got my routine down pat. My new routine. They still hadn't put anyone in the room with me. In fact, there had been no mention of it. I didn't like being there alone. So, I spent more time in the student center. It was better being around people—at first. I even got to know a few people in my classes. I never put more energy in them than I had to, though. It felt pointless. And I was just trying to get through the day. I had to reserve what energy I had.

***

Homesick

It is hard for me to write about this next part. Bear with me. Okay. Here I go ... Breathe.

So, I had a routine down pat. My parents had taught me order. It was my lifeline. I kept trying to eat healthy. I had less of an appetite, but it was helping to hold the pieces of my life together. Smoothie with protein powder in the student center every morning. I would grab a to-go salad there for lunch. An apple out of my mini-fridge every afternoon when I was done with classes. I kept packets of nuts in my backpack. They were like my pills. I would pull them out when my blood sugar felt low. Enough protein to get me to the next class. The next task. I tried to run, but my joints ached. My stomach began to hurt. I kept this burning sensation in my chest. I felt like I wasn't digesting my food anymore.

I even went to the school clinic one day because I had this lump in my throat that wouldn't go away. She weighed me. I was down twelve pounds. I knew my clothes were big on me. But twelve pounds? I was already fairly thin. I looked at myself naked in the mirror on the back of our bathroom door that night. I mean ... *my* bathroom door. I was a skeleton. The nurse didn't have any answers for me that day. But as I was rattling off my symptoms to her, I saw this look on her face. She had seen this many times being the nurse on a college campus for years. If she had known my normal weight, it would have been a referral to the counseling office, I'm sure.

I began to feel detached from everyone and everything on that campus. And I started having those feelings like I had when I first found out Flora was leaving. That sudden sinking feeling. Like doom. A foreboding. I would get these chills. My heart would start racing out of control. And an urge to run would overwhelm me ... from wherever I was ... class ... my car in traffic. Sometimes, I would feel like I couldn't breathe. Then afterwards, I would be so tired, and the sadness would be even more intense. It became a cycle. And I never knew when an attack was coming. That was the most terrifying part—the unpredictability. It felt like the only safe place was my bed. I couldn't wait to get in it every night. One night, my dad did his Friday call. I was already asleep for the night.

Friday calls were hard. I tried my best to fake a life. I played up my acquaintances in class like they were real friendships. I would complain about my professors— like I even cared. It took all the energy I had. But I didn't need the drama. They would make a big fuss if I was honest—especially if they knew about the weight loss. They might even demand I come home. That prospect was even worse. I kept trudging on ... getting enough of the basics done ... eating enough calories ... acting enough normal ... just so I could make it back to the safety of my bed.

At first, I still went to my spot on the eighth floor of the library. I had always been alone up there, so it didn't feel as abnormal. One day, the conditions were like the day the sparrow visited me. The sun was shining in my spot. I closed my eyes. I took a couple of deep breaths, said a prayer for help, and slowly opened my eyes. I wanted to see that sparrow. In fact, I begged God to see that sparrow. Anything. Any sign of hope. Any help I could get. But there was nothing but a cold concrete ledge. I sat there and just stared at it. I felt dead. Like a mound of useless flesh. A cloud eventually moved in, and my spot grew dark.

I remember thinking in that moment, *My pastor was right, wasn't he? I am worthless. Unworthy. Just a Jezebel. I'm finally getting my due punishment. He was right all along about God. God is cruel. He probably does burn people in hell for eternity. Maybe just for fun. And he doesn't love me. He never did. This is all just a cruel game.*

It wasn't long before I quit going to the library. I quit going to class. And I quit eating for the most part. I tried to get a shower every day even though they made me dizzy. The days and nights started blurring together. I would occasionally get messages on my Instagram from friends at home. That's how we stayed connected, I guess. Friendships held together by pointless reels. But I decided it was best if I just deleted my account. It took too much energy. They didn't seem to notice. I began ignoring Flora's texts. She probably just assumed I was upset with her and that it would pass with a little time and space.

The attacks didn't happen in my room. But my heart was still doing all these crazy things. Even in bed. Skipping beats. Pounding out of my chest sometimes. I knew it was probably partly dehydration because they would calm down when I drank water. I tried to make myself drink at least one bottle of tap water a day. On some level, I still held on to the order that had been ingrained in me growing up. My dad used to preach, "Routine is the key to a good life, Laine." This was no life. But I would do enough to survive. One bottle of water a day was my goal. I had a few boxes of graham crackers and granola bars in the room. A stale bag of popcorn by my bed. If I got some food in me, I would have really accomplished something that day. Just enough to stay alive. For what, I wasn't sure.

Then, on a Sunday morning, I heard a loud knock on my door. Voices. A man and a woman. I hadn't been to class in two weeks. And my phone was completely dead. I suddenly remembered that I hadn't answered my dad's

Friday night call. I opened the door. It was my advisor and campus police. She said softly, "Laine?" I'm sure I didn't even resemble the ambitious student she helped in her office. I nodded. The officer looked at me and back at her. She thanked him, and he walked away. She asked if she could come into my room. I suddenly felt ridiculous—self-conscious—like I wanted to do a quick outfit change, put some lip gloss on, and pretend this all wasn't really happening.

Mrs. Robinson. I remembered her immediately when I opened the door—although we had mostly emailed. She was a beautiful black woman. Dressed in a mossy green skirt suit and heels. I imagined, when I first met her, that she was in pageants when she was younger, with the way she held herself. And her majestic presence was a glaring light on my brokenness.

She said in almost a whisper, "Your parents are worried about you, Laine. And so are your friends."

I laughed and said, "What friends?"

She said, James and your ... your old roommate. Flor—" She struggled to remember her name.

I said, "Flora. It's Flora." Then, I broke completely open. I sat down on my bed. Sobbing. Moaning like a wounded animal. The sounds were shocking even to me. But I couldn't stop them. They just kept coming and coming. She just sat beside me with her hand gently on my bony back. I finally pulled myself together enough to say, "I just want to go home."

She replied, "We can arrange that. I think it would be best for you right now."

I corrected her, "No. I want to go home. My real home." She knew exactly what I meant.

Mrs. Robinson saved my life that day.

***

Daffodils

Of course, Mrs. Robinson had to go through the procedures. But I hadn't "made a plan." It was kind of a level two emergency situation, I guess. She recommended I call my parents. I did. She helped me get back to the nurse and in with a counselor. I got a low dose of antidepressant to help get me out of the hole. She emailed all my professors. They helped me come up with a plan to get back on track. My parents started reaching out every day. My dad started texting. He went nuts with the emojis. My mom would send funny memes or pictures of Gus. I knew that was their way of just making sure there was still life on the other end.

I'm not going to pretend things were suddenly normal. It was a process. But I started going back to class—partly because my advisor was checking to make sure I did. I called James and Flora. Her mom was doing better on the trial medication. Flora was trying to decide if she was going to come back the next year. It looked promising.

And we had some almost springlike days. I wasn't strong enough to run, but I started walking the track. I made sure I got enough calories. The color was back in my face. And I slowly started gaining the twenty pounds back that I lost. I wanted food again. I wanted to live.

My parents soon came for a week. We stayed together at a hotel nearby with an indoor lazy river. I took them to a nearby planetarium. They pretended to be fascinated with all my random facts. My mom, of course, wanted to spruce my room up a little. We shopped for a new comforter, and I took them to my favorite local restaurants. I showed them all around campus. Dad showed me where his dad's dorm had once stood—and the building where his dad met my grandmother. He, of course, had shown me when we did our first college visit and again when I moved in my dorm my freshman year, but I pretended like he hadn't.

It wasn't long before the daffodils were poking through the dead leaves. *Maybe Flora was right. Everything is going to be fine.* But first, I had a lesson coming my way. *Hold on for this one.*

Chapter 6

Up in Flames

My funds were getting low. I had planned to get a job immediately after Christmas break. It was past time— for a lot of reasons. I didn't want to just work anywhere. I wanted a professional-ish job. Maybe something in a hospital. I had graduate school ahead of me. And I hadn't tossed out the idea of medical school. Interest in alternative medicine was growing. And I thought that maybe by the time I graduated, there will be more openness in the field. Either way, I needed to decide.

I got my job quickly. I hesitantly used my marketing experience at Bill Marley's office to land it. I beefed it up. I still don't know if they called him for a reference. I probably wouldn't have been there if they did. Anyway, the job was in marketing at the hospital, as an assistant. Part-time. I helped set up booths at health fairs or community events. I did lots of clerical-like work. I rarely got to be around anything truly "medical" at first, but I was through the doors. It gave me a chance to observe the inner workings of a hospital.

I worked my days that I didn't have class and an occasional Saturday if something was going on in the community. My "office" was a small room in the basement not far from the morgue. It was close to where they stored their marketing materials. The hall used to be almost empty, and I just swore up and down that I heard things sometimes. I liked to find reasons to go upstairs. The real marketing office was near administration. *Too stuffy.* So, I would sit in the cafeteria when I was working on my laptop.

It was a teaching hospital and affiliated with the university. I used to watch the medical interns come in and out. They looked tired. I would wonder to myself if this was the life I really wanted. I mean ... that's just the beginning. It's all-consuming. But I watched them move through the food line and shovel their meal in before returning to their duties.

I noticed this one guy. Partly because he had a big personality that demanded it. He had an athletic build. Sandy hair. High energy type. Always seemed to be in a hurry to get to the next thing. He had a thick Southern accent—maybe even more Southern than my own. Oh, and he wore snakeskin cowboy boots ... with scrubs. I know. And I'm sure there's a rule against it or something. Anyway, I had seen him many times. He never really noticed me—not that I even cared at first. Then, one day, he sat down right next to me. I think it was a Tuesday, and he was eating taco salad. He was shoveling it in. I thought, *Dear Lord! He acts like he was born in a barn. How did he even get into med school?* I was a bit annoyed. Then, he got up to take his tray, and he did like a double take of me. I suddenly became self-conscious. Nervous. He smiled slowly. I broke eye contact as soon as I could. For some reason, I was reminded of Gus when he spotted a defenseless bird outside.

I saw him frequently after that. I'm not going to lie. I kind of started looking for him. And I may or may not have started going to the bathroom near my office before going upstairs. A touch of lip gloss. Maybe some eye drops and a stroke of mascara if I had stayed up too late studying. My hair was still in-between. But I had learned to pull my bangs back in a twist or a braid. *It would do.* As the weeks went by, I noticed that any time he was with the other interns, he was at front and center. They would sit around him like they had bought tickets to his private stand-up show. I wanted to move closer to see what was so funny. I missed laughing, and I was intrigued by him and his snakeskin cowboy boots.

One day, I was putting some boxes of materials in the marketing director's van out front. He charged out of the doors like a bull. He saw me. My body tightened. I was thinking, *Go on ... please just go on.* Instead, he stopped and threw his backpack on the ground. He said,

"I'll get those. They are too heavy for you." He put them in the van and walked away. It all happened so quickly that I didn't even speak. It was like a cat had my tongue—exactly like that.

It wasn't long after that I saw him in the ER—doing his thing. I had to deliver something to the chaplain's office about a service our hospice was doing for the community. I think this is when I fell, and I fell hard. He was laser-focused. Quick. Smart. He was completely invested in this patient just coming in on a gurney off an ambulance. He and another doctor were barking out orders. Staff twice his age hanging on every word. It was clear to me, in that second, how he made it into medical school. This guy was a force. He was no pond frog. I didn't know where he dwelled. I just knew that I wanted to find out.

Now, again, I didn't go all crazy. I remembered what Gram taught me. *I am the flower.* I knew he had taken notice of me already. But I dialed it up a bit. I bought a few cute dresses. I got up a little earlier on the days that I worked. I started thinking about him when I wasn't there. And he must have been thinking about me too. He came into the cafeteria one day. I was sitting there on my laptop, pretending I didn't notice. He came over before even getting his tray and said, "Where were you Tuesday?" I stopped. "Tuesday?" He said, "Yeah ... you usually work Tuesdays ... right?" My heart was racing. I felt almost dizzy. Probably because I quit breathing. As he turned and walked away, he grinned and said, "You thought I didn't notice?" If any other guy in that hospital had just said that to me, I would have been completely creeped out. I might even have a little chat with security. But this was like I had just been dipped into some kind of intoxicant. And I wanted more. "Love drunk," my Gram used to call it.

It wasn't long before he would come sit next to me whenever he had a chance. I found out his name. Dylan. And no surprise. He was also from the Deep South. So, we had a lot to talk about. Of course, school and whether I should go into medicine. And no doubt—he was funny. And smart. He was much smarter than I was. He was one of those people who seemed to know some about any subject. Current events ... he's on it. History ... ask him anything. He was well-read. He was much more well-rounded with his genres. He loved the classics, poetry, Greek mythology. I was no match. I was in checkmate.

Dylan was a showman. I kind of felt like if he ever asked me to hang out, it would be in some kind of melodramatic way—not over tacos in that sterile cafeteria. Sure enough, I went to my car one afternoon, and there was a note. At first, I thought it was a parking ticket. But I was parked in my normal spot. I flipped it over, and on a script, he had written, "One dinner with

Dylan. Call me in the morning." His cell phone number was on the bottom of it along with an exaggerated messy doctor signature. I got in my car and smiled all the way back to campus. How your whole life can change so quickly. I was sure glad I held on for this chapter of it.

That was our first date. I felt like the luckiest girl in the world. And it was just like I had imagined. He opened the door for me. He had a "first date" playlist for the car. We went to a dimly lit restaurant that I was not sure he could even afford. He acted like I shouldn't even have to order for myself. That was *his* job. I was too dainty to raise my pretty little head from my menu and talk to the waiter. He made sure I was happy with the meal—and the company. Not like at work, we talked about more intimate things, and if the conversation ever veered away from me, he would bring it right back. "What's your favorite memory growing up? Tell me about your parents. How do you feel about this or that?" *Ummmm ... how do I feel? Feel? Well, this is different.* Will never cared how I *felt* about anything. I had never had someone so interested in learning me. He would just study my face and smile as I gluttonously went on and on about myself.

And there was usually a twist or a surprise to our dates. Never boring. One night, he borrowed a roommate's motorcycle and picked me up from the dorm. He gave me a quick lesson on the do's and don'ts of being a passenger.

He helped me on and gently swiped the stray hair out of my face as he put on my helmet. When I was all set, he kissed me on the nose. Then, he took off for the interstate like a bat out of hell. We drove for miles and miles passing every single car as I held on for dear life.

And once he borrowed the same roommate's Jeep and packed a cooler of food. Cheese, chocolate, wine. We drove to a lookout. We went to the spot to eat and watch the sunset, and he walked me down a little trail, gently holding my hand and watching my every step. We sat on a giant boulder until the stars came out. They were magnificent away from the city lights. And, of course, he knew almost as much about astronomy as I did. Although not more. I taught him how constellations were identified in Ancient Egypt. And how there are now eighty-eight official constellations that have been named. And how most people think the Big Dipper and Little Dipper are constellations, but they are actually just part of constellations. And how the word constellation means "set with stars." He said, "Set with stars. Like us." I said, "Yes ... exactly like us."

Dylan always dropped me off back at the dorm. Always a goodnight kiss. And I had only been kissed by a pond frog. These were different. Full of raw passion. The kind of passion they write poetry and songs about. The kind of passion that makes people go crazy like the fools in Romeo and Juliet. They were like he was just going to consume my whole being right there. But he had this gentleness at the very same time. An almost old-fashioned regard for me. It's a deadly mix.

Coming to my dorm room was beneath him. That was never said but understood. But there was never any pressure to go to his apartment. I assumed it was because three other guys lived there. *Probably a pigsty.* And he always had some reason to need to get back. Dylan was always busy.

I always tried to look the part. Feminine. Fragile even. I had never been the damsel in distress. I surprised myself how well I played the role. Dylan made me want to be saved. He made me want to rock babies and make potatoes *au gratin* every day. All day for the rest of my life. And anything else he wanted of me. *Anything.*

But I kind of felt like an imposter. He didn't know how difficult I could be—he didn't know that my friends that I talked about back home were barely acquaintances now. I actually had no close friends except James and Flora. And James and Flora never knew about him. He didn't know I was seeing a counselor. I didn't want him to know. Any of it. I was always aware of the fact that he was falling for a version of what I thought he wanted me to be. I didn't care. I'll be that. Just give me time. *His hobbies would be my hobbies. His people would be my people.*

It was kind of like we were a couple. I guess. Sometimes. But our lunches in the cafeteria were the closest thing we had to "real life." Rushed lunches under fluorescent lights. Schedules and responsibilities. Our dates were more like prom dates. We didn't sit up at night to talk on the phone like I had with Will in the early days. We didn't even talk every day. It was different. But Dylan was in a whole different stage of life than Will. So, my expectations should be. Right? I mean ... he was a full-fledged grown up. And he was slammed busy. Always busy. He got lots of passes for that. As many passes as he wanted.

I still had moments of anxiety. My counselor had been doing breath work with me. I was also in a yoga class that taught relaxation. I was in a pretty good place though—if the only gauge was my "mood." Those endorphins were working double time. I didn't want food again. Not because I didn't want to live, but because I was too busy, happy, and nervous to bother. My hunger pangs were replaced by the flutters of gigantic butterflies. My grades were not great. I definitely wasn't the stellar student that came to campus that first semester. And my parents understood I was still "struggling." But they didn't really know *why*. The real reason now. My classes were just a side note. My trips to the eighth floor of the library were non-existent. I no longer cared if I saw the sparrow—or what the seekers and thinkers wrote in those books. Not unless Dylan wrote them.

We hadn't talked about future plans. He would be leaving for home the middle of June. I was going to stay the summer to keep my job. And then back to school in the fall. My parents agreed to supplement my pay to help me afford an apartment. As June got closer, Dylan didn't slack on his efforts in pursuing me. Our lunches moved outside in the sunshine. Sometimes, he would need to "get something from his car" in the parking garage. I would go with him; he would grab me and kiss me like he needed me to breathe. I would have to literally come back down to Earth before I went back to work.

Then one day, it was like an out of body experience. After one of his kisses, he asked me to go away with him for the weekend. This was the next step. I would finally get a glimpse of his world. Of course, Dylan-like, the location was a surprise.

I started obsessing in the mirror. I got a manicure and pedicure. A waxing. That was a first. I deep-conditioned my hair. I exfoliated my entire body multiple times. And began planning my wardrobe for the trip. This required his participation. Athletic wear? Bathing suit? Hiking boots? Ski bibs? You literally never knew with Dylan. We could be flying to the Congo for all I knew. He enjoyed the tease. He would give me impossible clues and watch me suffer. The trips to his car were more frequent. The kisses were more passionate—if that were even possible.

This wasn't love drunk. This was harder than liquor. Dylan was a Schedule I narcotic.

I hadn't told anyone about Dylan. I surely hadn't told my parents. The relationship was still so ambiguous. And almost like a fantasy. And how do you tell your dad that you met this really hot intern in snakeskin cowboy boots that makes you crazy, and he's whisking you away for a mystery weekend. How do you tell him that without him driving eleven hours to meet this "young man" first. Well, I'll tell you how. You don't. You lie your pants off.

We were leaving for a trip on Friday after my last class. I went ahead and called Dad. I left a message. "Hey ... going out with friends. Ummm ... just wanted to touch base before I left ... in case I didn't hear my phone." *Okay ... that's over.*

We would only be gone two nights, but I packed everything under the sun. I was a nervous wreck. He'd never seen me not made up. Uggghh ... morning breath. And of course, I knew that there was a one thousand percent chance that we would finally be together ... like ... in the "biblical sense."

Friday about six o'clock, Dylan texted a photo of himself in front of the dorm. His sunglasses down on his nose. "Can you help me, ma'am? I'm lost." I played along

... "I'll be more than happy to show you the way, Sir. I'll be right down." I got my colossal bright yellow suitcase on the elevator and rolled it out to his car. We started dying laughing.

I said, "Don't make fun. It's easy to spot at the airport."

He asked as he was putting it into the back of his car, "What do you have in here? Your furniture?? All of your textbooks…since grade school??"

We got in the car. He kissed me gently and said, "I really just have one question. Do you have a bathing suit in that big yellow suitcase, ma'am?"

I went on nervously. "Well, I actually have two ... a navy one-piece and a white bikini. I hate the one-piece. I have always had trouble finding one to fit me. It's my long torso. I have to—"

He stopped me mid-sentence with one of those other kisses—the crazy-making kind—and said, "All you need is that bikini but probably not for long."

Still not sure where we were going, I got a text. Dad was sending all these emojis in response to my message. I replied with a string of hearts. *That's a relief. No questions.* We hit the interstate going north. Dylan rolled down both of our windows and turned the radio up. I put my feet on the dash and threw my arm out the window into the wind. I said, "Take me anywhere. Just make sure you feed me and tell me I'm pretty."

About an hour later, we pulled up at a marina. I wasn't expecting to get there so quickly. I said, "Oh ... where are we sleeping? The deck of a boat?" He replied, "No, silly. I am going to feed you and tell you that you are beautiful." Then, suddenly he took a different tone. "In fact, you are the most beautiful girl I've ever known, Laine." I rolled my eyes. He held my face and looked at me with a seriousness I had not seen in him. "No, really. I mean it." We barely made it out of the car with our clothes intact. I wondered if there was such a thing as dying of happiness. If so, my death was imminent.

We got a table outside, overlooking the water. Boats were coming in for the night. A candle flickered on the table with a gentle warm breeze. There was a band, but they were winding down. Our food took forever. We didn't care. Dylan held my hand across the table and hung on my every word. Most people had left by the time we finished our meal. He said, "Wanna see those stars again?" He paid and told me he had to run to the car. He took forever, then came back, took the keys out of his pocket, and put them on the table. They weren't his car keys though. He walked me to a slip without saying a word and helped me on a boat. At the back near the captain's chair was my suitcase and a quilt. He made some joke about how the suitcase would probably sink the boat, but we would go down "full and deliriously happy." Then, he brought the quilt over and set it next to me before pulling the boat out of the slip.

From a dark, quiet cove, we saw the stars. Every one of them.

The boat belonged to a resident's parents. And the lake house, that turned out to be my surprise destination, belonged to them too. Dylan was right. A bathing suit was about all I needed. And we didn't do much swimming. Will and I had only been practicing being grown ups. Our encounters were awkward and guilt-ridden. This was not Dylan's first rodeo—probably not his hundred and first either. This was a whole different experience, and the whole weekend was like a dream. As I stretched out in the couple's big bed of down pillows and high thread-count sheets with massive windows overlooking the lake, I imagined what my life would be like with Dylan. It was more than I had ever let myself dream of wanting. Dylan was an ocean dweller. No doubt. Dylan ruled the whole ocean.

The weekend went too quickly. The night we got back, after my shower, I tossed Gram's advice right out of the window. I texted him. "Goodnight. Thank you again for the incredible weekend. Went by way too fast. Oh. And by the way. I'm in love with you." I sat there smiling and anxiously waiting for his response. I'm pretty sure Will told me he loved me first. Almost certain of it. This was brave. Dylan made me feel brave.

Invincible even. So, I sat there on my bed in a towel, with a smile on my face, waiting on some quip and the confirmation that he loved me back. *He might make me work for it, but he definitely will say it back.*

Yes. Dylan the entertainer "in the snakeskin cowboy boots" was madly in love with me too. Ready to spend his forever with me. I know ... stupid.

I can hear Gram now. "Don't believe the lies you tell yourself, child."

My phone was eerily silent. I set it down and finished getting ready for bed. Still nothing. I talked myself out of what I felt like was happening. *He probably had something he had to do at the hospital. Probably up to his elbows in blood and IV tubing right now. Yep ... that's it. Oh ... or I just wore him out. He probably fell asleep. Poor guy. He will make some joke about it in an early morning text ... along with his "I love you more." Something like that. He was an 'I love you more" kind of guy. It would become another competition ... who loved the other the most. It would probably become "our thing."*

The next day ... nothing until around noon. I guess he knew he had to reply something eventually. My heart was racing as I pressed on his text. "Hey ... great weekend. Hit those books ... Dr. Anderson. Finals coming up." That was it. His whole tone completely different. It was more like a high five to a guy you played a round of golf with—

not a woman whom you shared a bed with all weekend and worshipped twenty-four hours ago.

I decided to act like this was totally normal human behavior. I gave him a thumbs up. Then my heart sank before it broke. I finally understood the word "heartbroken." I was completely heartbroken with a case of whiplash. *How can someone change that quickly? Unless ... unless ... he didn't. Was that all an act? If so, he deserved an Oscar. He deserved all the awards ... including selfish asshole of the year.*

That Tuesday, I didn't see him. Thursday rolled around. He came into the cafeteria. He was casually eating a pack of crackers. "Too busy for lunch." Swore he would catch me that weekend. He was "slammed in the ER." Then, that weekend, he got called in ... and, after his shift, he promised one of the other interns he would help him with his laptop. It "took all weekend to fix it." That weekend turned into promises for the next.

You know the drill. I had seen the drill—from afar, at least. Excuse after stupid excuse.

But I was too smart for this. This wasn't me dammit ... who I was. And I realized, I didn't even know who he was. My login wasn't working for Instagram, and I had deleted the app on my phone. So, I used the Instagram I had made for Bill Marley's office. Finally, I found Dylan. Public. Old photo—hadn't posted in over a year. I scrolled through the accounts he followed. Attractive female ... after attractive female ... after attractive female. He definitely had a "type." And I fit it. I felt like I could vomit. Literally.

I have a theory about these guys. They don't *love* women. Maybe just the opposite. It's their game. Cat and mouse. In this case, catch and release. He had stalked me like prey. Calculating. Outsmarted me at every turn. That was part of the thrill. The hunt and the capture. This part was probably satisfying too—playing with his injured prey. He didn't want to learn me. He didn't care about my life. He was grooming me. I struggled to find "grace" for this predator. Maybe if I had walked into that ER, Jezebel style, and had given him an earful right in front of the staff. But I knew I would have just looked like the crazy one. And I had to work with these people. *I need this job.*

I did have the opportunity to retaliate. He gave it to me himself. First time, I actually thought he had already left town. And I got the expected "I miss you" text. I immediately started my reply. Paragraphs—correctly punctuated and spell-checked. A whole thesis on why he was a jerk. A piece of my mind. *I will show him that he's not messing with some twit here.* But before I hit send, I backed out of every paragraph. I deleted it. All of it.

Sometimes, silence speaks the loudest. I wanted him to hear me loud and clear. But it continued to eat me alive. The feeling of being had ... duped ... used. Discarded like trash. On the podcast that I listened to about soulmates, the expert said, a "karmic relationship"—sometimes a "twin flame"—will come in like a tornado and wreck your life." Exciting at first. But often a tumultuous end. Like Romeo and Juliet. I had definitely been tornadoed, manipulated, had, used, poisoned, pierced with a dagger. All of it.

Chapter 7

Humble Pie

Grades came out. I did better on my finals than I expected. I had been looking for an apartment and finally found an inexpensive one in the upstairs of an old white Victorian near campus. It was full of light. There was a gigantic oak tree in the front yard. I loved it and couldn't wait to make it feel like mine. I took a week off work to go home and get some things. I could fit lamps and a side table in my back seat. A few things in the trunk. My parents would bring furniture later.

I wasn't in a great place emotionally. But I had tools now. I was doing the breathing my yoga teacher taught me. Hand on your heart ... four seconds in ... hold seven seconds ... eight seconds out. I was eating healthy. I talked through the Dylan saga with my counselor. She talked to me about self-love and forgiveness. How it's important to offer people that—but also ourselves when we make mistakes—and sometimes more importantly ourselves. I remember she said, "What would you say to your best friend if this had happened to her?" I said,

"I would give her all of the comfort and grace I had to offer, of course." Then she said, "Now, offer the same to yourself." Still some of the best advice I've ever gotten.

I left for home before dawn to be there for dinner. I pulled in the driveway. There was a big black Jeep-like vehicle behind Mom's car. It was one of those that looked like it was issued by the military. You know the ones. *Like are you going to war at the Piggly Wiggly, people?* Anyway, I parked on the other side. I walked in, and there was "the gang." The girls were downstairs watching a movie. Mom and Patricia were baking peach pies in the kitchen. And Dad and Jeff were out on the back deck grilling hamburgers. I thought, *Mom didn't tell me about their visit because she was afraid I would cancel my plans. Thanks, Mom.* This was our first encounter since I wrecked Christmas. I tried to act excited. My Aunt Patricia looked at me differently. Not the proud aunt look. The "bless your heart and I know absolutely everything about every mistake you have ever made in your life" aunt look. Sisters talk. They hold nothing back. I immediately knew that she knew. And I also knew that Jeff knew because sisters also tell their husbands everything. They knew about my breakdown. They knew about my grades. I thanked God they didn't know about Dylan. That would have sent me right over the edge.

Dad heard me pull in, and he and Jeff came in the back door. My dad gave me a hug, studied my face, smiled at me, and hugged me again. Jeff stood there with an empty glass in his hand with this smug look of satisfaction on his face. He said, "Well, welcome home, scholar." He took the pitcher of tea out of the fridge and sat down at the island. Just reveling in my misfortune. I walked over—took the pitcher—and poured the tea for him. "Here let me do it for you. This thing always gives me a fit ... just spills everywhere." Suddenly. There was that look. The look that guy had on his face when James gave him the bag of cookies. Surprise? Embarrassment? Humility? It didn't matter. I went to my room to start packing.

A couple of weeks later, my parents rented a moving truck and delivered some larger pieces of furniture and boxes. We shopped for a new mattress. I contemplated asking them to bring Gus to live with me. But he was so happy there. He had his beat around the yard. I didn't want him confined. I also think my dad secretly liked having him around. So, the summer was busy setting up house. "Padding my nest," Gram called it.

Flora's mom was back on her feet. James and Flora came over and brought "housewarming presents" when they came to town. A bottle of red wine. And a book for my kitchen that broke down the nutritional value of just about any fruit or vegetable on the planet. I told Flora that was *our* book and that somebody had stolen the idea. We laughed. Then James said, "Oh ... I forgot something." He ran out to the car. He brought back a rectangle package wrapped in brown Kraft paper. I opened it. It was a wooden sign. It read "The Gathering Place." My heart swelled a thousand times its size.

Time to go back to class came soon enough. I was a junior. And I had a lot of catching up to do. I desperately needed to get my GPA back up if I was going to have any chance of applying to graduate school. I felt like I was up for the challenge. Things felt like they had almost come full circle. I had the resolve and the drive of the student that first stepped foot on that campus. And, although a bit weathered, I was stronger and smarter. Smarter in ways that really mattered.

That first day back, I went up to the eighth floor of the library. I didn't have any assignments or tests to study for yet. I sat down in my sunny spot. I closed my eyes. I put my hand on my heart and breathed ... four seconds in ... hold seven ... eight seconds out. But instead of opening my eyes to look for the sparrow, I kept them closed. I felt grateful. I felt God. Within me. Rebellious me. Confused me. Lost me. Angry me. Unwise me. God had been within me all along. Through it all.

One night, I unpacked a few of the boxes my parents brought. One was full of books. Some went into a pile to put in the donation box at the community library. I wouldn't dare throw a book away. A few went on my mantle. Two books of poetry went on my nightstand. And at the bottom of the box was my Gram's Bible. I ran my fingers across her name in gold on the right bottom corner. I held it to my chest. I had such a contentious relationship with this book. But not her. I vowed that in her memory, I would try again. *Maybe I had more spiritual eyes. More mature eyes. Maybe I would see it differently now.*

Chapter 8

Resonance

I was in the storage room near my office when I heard the whistling. I was boxing up some brochures for an event that Saturday and didn't pay any attention at first. Then, I thought this person was going in and out of my office. I walked down the hall to find out. My calculations were wrong. He was going in and out of the empty office beside mine. I caught a glimpse of the back of him as he turned to go to the door to the parking garage. It wasn't long before I was working in my office, and here came the whistling again. I stepped out into the hallway. There was this guy—maybe thirty—probably just over five feet tall. Strawberry blond hair. Baggy khakis and with the sleeves of his blue dress shirt rolled up. He's maneuvering some large-framed posters. He didn't see me. He was in his own world.

I went over to help him with the door. He almost jumped out of his skin. We both died laughing.

"Did you think I was the ghost?"

He said, "Oh we have a ghost? Goodie. I just love a good ghost. What is his name?"

"He remains unnamed. We've been waiting on you to name him." He set the frames down and pondered like he was taking the task very seriously.

Then, he said, "I've got nothing. I really need to get to know him first. Wait. How do you know it's a *him*?"

I knew immediately that I had a playmate. And I had known this person a million lifetimes. It was like putting on your favorite sweater—or sliding into your slippers where the grooves of every toe are perfectly worn.

We finally did our "introductions." I found out his name was Gabe and that they had moved some of the hospice employees to the building. He was the volunteer coordinator for both the inpatient and outpatient hospices.

I started spending more time in my office down there with the good company next door. At first, he would just pop in to talk about something going on in the hospital— or just to see how I was doing. Not in the manipulative way, like Dylan, but in a real and genuine way. There was nothing to gain from this friendship—except friendship. It was so refreshingly innocent and uncomplicated. Sometimes, I would grab him a coffee from upstairs. He might pick up a croissant and bring it to me. He knew that was about the only thing that I liked in the cafeteria. I loved to hear him whistling coming off the elevator and down that once dark and dreary hallway. He lit it up like a Christmas tree. Always happy. It was contagious.

Gabe and I started eating our lunch together when we both happened to be there. I would gripe about the cafeteria food and how we were supposed to be a place to heal. I would say, "You can't heal on powdered eggs and Jell-O." I was so passionate about my convictions. He would say something like he had actually read that powdered eggs were curing rare diseases all over the world. Anything to jab me. But I would bring my fresh fruit, homemade hummus, raw vegetables, salads, olives, good cheese, iced herbal teas. It was my way of rebelling against that gross cafeteria. Gabe would bring his simple sandwich made of highly processed sandwich meat on white bread and maybe a bag of chips, but he would munch on a celery stick if I forced him. He would say, "Okay, I'll eat this rabbit food just to make you happy ... and to keep you quiet."

One day, we were having lunch, and Gabe confided in me about his health. He said, "I should probably tell you something about me. I'm ... well, I'm ... defective."

I laughed, "Defective? Tell me something I don't know." He chuckled. But I could tell by his face that the conversation was getting ready to take a different turn. And I could tell that he did not want to be talking about any of it.

He said, "I was born with heart and kidney abnormalities. I mean ... there is nothing I can do about it outside of organ transplants, but I'm not a candidate. Most days, I don't even think about it."

I put down my lunch. "Gabe, are you serious? There's nothing funny about that. Are you sure ... are you sure there is nothing that can be done? Medicine has come a long way since you were born."

He said, "Laine, I have the best doctors there are in both fields. I've lived longer than was expected. They kind of consider me to be a miracle. But you always knew that. Didn't you? That I'm a miracle." He batted his eyelashes.

But I wasn't laughing. I put my face in my hands for a second. And then looked at him. "Gabe. Dammit."

Then, very Gabe-like, he said, "They have attributed my long life to white bread and bologna."

I wadded up my napkin and threw it at him. He wasn't going to allow any pity. Not an ounce. The only thing that I could do for him was respect his wishes.

But genuinely, even the prospect of death seemed trivial to Gabe. Gabe lived smack-dab in the middle of the moment. No regrets. No fear of the future. He was so alive and present. Somehow, I had no fear of his future either.

***

Baggage

I told Gabe about Dylan. I have to admit that I was replaying it all in my head on a daily basis. Obsessing. I would find any way that I could to work it into our conversations. He always gave me his full attention.

But one day, he said, "Well. Okay. What did you learn from it?"

"Ummm. I learned how to spot a player from a mile away—or at least from across a cafeteria." We laughed.

Then, he got kind of serious. And he said, "Did the experience humble you?" He knew the answer.

I said, "Well, no doubt."

"Well, then, you just have to see it as a gift. Dylan gave you the gift of humility, Lainey. Thank him."

I always told him he was channeling Gram when he called me "Lainey." Maybe that's why I always listened so intently to his advice.

Another day, I once again had managed to sneak the topic of Dylan into our conversation, Gabe said, "I wonder why Dylan feels the need to manipulate women?" What do you think he has gone through? Do you know anything about his relationship with his family? How about his mother?"

I said, "Ha. Dylan?" I couldn't imagine him being wounded or vulnerable to anyone or anything.

"Maybe that bravado is just a costume, Laine. Maybe he has to put it on to cover up the wounded child inside of it. Maybe someone hurt him deeply as a child."

I said, "Uggghhh stop it ... stop trying to make me feel sorry for him, Gabe." Dylan didn't deserve one droplet of grace. I wanted Gabe's sympathy. Dylan wasn't deserving of it. And even the suggestion of it infuriated me. It felt like Gabe was siding with him.

But what Gabe knew was that seeing Dylan this way would benefit me even more than Dylan. It didn't let him off the hook. It let *me* off the hook. It would allow me to see him on a soul level— truly forgive him—which would allow me to finally let go. My burden would be lighter. Maybe this is what Jesus meant when he said, "Give away all that you own and follow me." Not literally give away our "stuff," but give away your attachments. All of them. Maybe he meant for us to give away our addictions, people, outcomes—our grudges too. Maybe we can't take our heavy baggage on our spiritual journeys.

I had been thinking more about some of Jesus' teachings. With a lot of resistance, I had started trying to read a little out of Gram's Bible. One night, I noticed she had underlined twice, with an asterisk beside it where Jesus said, "The kingdom of God is within you." As I sat with those words that I had read a hundred times, I realized for the first time that I experienced this on the eighth floor of the library. The kingdom within that doesn't depend on location or circumstances. It's a state of mind. I thought—*what if hell is within too*? I know I've lived in my own hell on a cheap mattress in a dorm room not far from here. And I kept reliving the hell of being used and discarded by Dylan. I was stuck there. Half in and half out. In my own self-made purgatory. Putting myself through the experience of it over and over.

***

Sweet Release

One afternoon, I went to get Gabe and myself a soda. He had been the bad influence. I always called it rat poison when he would go get one. It tickled him when I would give in to him. As I was coming down the hall with our drinks, he was talking to a girl outside of his office. I slowed my pace to give them time to wrap up their conversation.

She walked away, and I sat down in his office and popped open my can. He said, "Look at you ... so wild and crazy. Living on the edge." Then, Gabe said, "That was Rebecca. Gather all the grace you can muster when you meet her. All of it." I was confused. He went on to explain that she also worked for hospice and would be using his office some. Of course, in all our deep dives, I had told Gabe about my upbringing. He knew that there had been a wound there too. And he knew that I had a propensity for telling people off. I asked him what he meant about Rebecca. Gabe took an apple slice from my lunch and said, "Just be gentle with her, Laine. Seriously." Like James and Flora, Gabe wouldn't spill the tea on someone. This is why I felt so free to share my stories with him. My stories were safe with Gabe and so were Rebecca's.

Flora had returned to school. She and James were doing the dorm life again this year. By the time I met Rebecca, we had several meals at my apartment. We stayed true to our tradition. The beet was the veggie of the hour. Beet soup, roasted beets, and beet hummus. I loved my little apartment. I decorated with lots of creams and white, pillows and throws. I put fairy lights in my kitchen window. Just beneath my "Gathering Place" sign. James suggested we put flashing neon lights around the sign itself. I said, "Like a truck stop?" Flora said, "We could do a whole thing on truck stop fare—like those pickled eggs in a jar." I added, "Yeah, and we could do a science experiment on them while we are at it."

I was seeing my counselor less. I had gotten off the antidepressant. The breathing exercises were just part of my every day. I usually did them as I was falling asleep. Definitely did them when I felt a bit frazzled. And I tried to have a few minutes a day to meditate. I use the term loosely. My brain is too active for true meditation. My counselor introduced me to healing frequencies. I listened to them with my earbuds when I felt particularly stressed or when I was studying for an exam. I learned that I could tap into that place I found on the eighth floor of the library any place I wanted. The kingdom within. No library or cathedral required.

And speaking of cathedrals, one day, I was upstairs in the hospital. I went up to put a flier on the community board near the chapel. I had never been in the chapel. I snuck inside. It was dark. Only the front lit up with an accent light on the large brass cross. I was alone, so I decided to sit for a minute. I took a deep breath. I wondered if I would ever be a member of a church again. The thought of it made me feel kind of panicky. I know it may sound silly. Maybe not. But I think that kids who are especially sensitive can be kind of traumatized by religion. Think about it. God loves you, but will, without hesitation, burn you in hell for eternity if all the boxes aren't checked. Or yes, two plus two equals four, but you had better not even challenge the literal interpretation of these stories that make no logical sense. It can be confusing to a kid. And yes—maybe traumatizing for some.

I sat there thinking about my own church experience. *Was it even really that traumatic? I don't even know.* The other kids in my church seemed unbothered. *Maybe I had been the one doing the traumatizing.* But I thought about people who had pain so deep that they never could even step foot in a church again. Like a girl, from my hometown who was forced to sit by her stepfather every Sunday morning on a hard pew in a church similar to mine— after he had molested her with liquor on his breath that Saturday night. Sunday morning, he would remind her that God had instructed him to "teach her about womanhood." That's a double whammy. The father and your stepfather teaming up on you. Raped Saturday night and threatened with the fiery torment on Sunday morning. And if the story couldn't be more tragic, she finally told, and her mother chose her new husband over her. She was forced to go live with her grandparents. She would never return to a pew. I was sure of it. And I wouldn't blame her if she didn't. But I hoped she had found the kingdom within. She had experienced enough hell on earth.

I took several more deep breaths. It felt holy in there. Removed from the world. No sermons about a fiery hell had been preached in that place. I thought about all the prayers that had been offered up right there. Thousands. Millions maybe. A hospital is like a little universe all its own. You can step on the elevator and have one person to your left celebrating a new life—and at the very same time to your right—have someone grieving the end of one. This chapel had cradled the souls experiencing those—and all of those in between. Those barely hanging on—looking for some sign of hope. Looking for their sparrow. Lots of those. I decided to offer my own prayers. I prayed for Gabe and his work. I prayed for my parents. I thanked God for them. I prayed for James and Flora. I prayed that I would know which direction to go with graduate school—to somehow know my purpose. Some kind of sign. Any kind. But one that would leave me with no doubt.

I sat for a minute. Took a few more deep breaths. I put my hand on my heart ... four seconds in ... hold seven ... eight seconds out. And I said a prayer for Dylan. "God help him heal whatever it is …" I didn't even know how to finish the prayer. So, I just thanked God for the lesson. And I thanked Dylan for the lesson. I released him— which released me. *It felt like heaven.*

Chapter 9

Storm Clouds

Gabe was putting together a training session for new volunteers. He asked for my help. The department approved it. I had never had any personal experience with death except for losing my grandmothers. My grandfathers had both already passed when I was born. My dad's mother had moved four hours away. We rarely saw her, and I barely remembered her funeral. My Gram—whole other story. But her death came very quickly. A diagnosis in the late fall, and she died on New Year's Eve. I wasn't close to her death. My parents protected me from it. But she was in so much pain we were all ready to let her go.

I do remember going to the hospital right after she died. My mom and my Aunt Patricia were in the room with her. My dad and I had come for a visit. The nurse stopped us in the hall and informed us that she had just passed away minutes before. I remember being so nervous as my dad slowly opened the door. She and I had such a strong bond that I thought that I would feel like part of me was gone too. But all I can say is that I had this overwhelming sense of peace. There was palpable peace and joy in that room. It was strange. I sensed her soul was at some kind of reunion. A homecoming of sorts. Death didn't feel scary at all.

Gabe and I tried to find a weekend to do the training where there were no big football games or community events. We finally decided on one in November. He had done many training sessions. But their numbers had dropped significantly. He wanted to make this one a little special. We got a budget, and we started the planning. Rebecca would be our clerical support. I was marketing. Gabe was the content creator.

My experience with Rebecca had still been minimal. Gabe suggested we use our lunches to start the planning. And I was only there in the hospital two days a week. So, I suggested we meet at my apartment for dinner some nights when I didn't have homework. Gabe taunted me by saying he would bring the bologna. I told him I had a strict no bologna rule in my house. He laughed. But I was more than apprehensive about working that closely with Rebecca. Gabe had been so vague. I didn't know what to expect. I treaded carefully anytime I had to deal with her.

I heard somewhere… if you think you've healed from your "stuff," go back to the scene of the crime. If you can and not fall back into old patterns, you probably have. If you have more work to do, that place ... those people ... whatever it was will stir it all right back up.

You can probably guess what's getting ready to happen here.

Like I said, my contact with Rebecca was minimal. I made sure of it. And as we had her join us for lunch, I didn't find anything particularly challenging at first. She was a little older. Dressed better. No doubt about that. She spent a lot of money at the mall. Very put together. "Nary a hair out of place," as my Gram used to say. She was in school working on a paralegal degree. Quick, efficient, and reliable. Somebody you wanted on your team in the office.

We were cordial. Polite even. Gabe seemed to have relaxed into the idea that we were going to get along just fine. But our demons soon began to tango. I mean ... we still maintained our cordiality. But there was a storm brewing. I could feel it. Soon, there was some passive aggressiveness being exchanged—with smiles on our faces. That's the worst kind. It feels so icky. "Oh no ... you were talking first ... please finish your thought. Oh no, you first ... that's a great idea ... I was just thinking ..." All the while, you just want to poke their eyes out. I almost would rather just have Jezebel deal with her. *She hates me. So what? Who cares?* But Gabe. This was so important to him. And I wanted him to be proud of me. I had come so far. Right?

The first showdown came when I suggested we have online or paper registration for the classes. A choice. A lot of volunteers were older. I just felt it would be more accommodating. Well, you would have thought I had recommended they come there in horse and buggy. Gabe agreed with Rebecca for the sake of not having to keep up with the paperwork that we would just do online. I think we went back and forth with it for a solid week. I didn't really care. But my big fat hairy ego did. And hers did too. And hers may have done a dance right there in my living room when Gabe finally declared a winner and went with her idea. I know … who even cares. But every stupid decision was like that. With smiles on our faces, our egos were in full-on battle.

***

The Good Father

Gabe was so easy to be around. Maybe because his ego had been unraveled by his health challenges. Maybe he never had a big problem with his ego in the first place. I do know he never had to "deconstruct" his own belief system. No need. He said his father welcomed his questions and his own interpretations.

Gabe was adopted at birth by an older couple. His mother was an artist and worked from her studio at home. His father was a professor of New Testament at a nearby private college. Gabe said that when he was a child, they attended a beautiful, old stone church with stained glass windows and arched wooden doorways. He loved going there. Gabe said that the minister had bushy white eyebrows, a big belly, and a thunderous laugh. They had a congregational cat named "Wafer." And vegetable and rose gardens out back that were tended to by all the regulars there. He said he remembered so much joy in that place.

But some Sundays, they would do something outdoors instead of attending service. It was there that his father taught him a lot of life lessons. Gabe's father taught him a reverence for every living thing. He said that his father seemed to approach the outdoors as reverently as he did their sanctuary.

They lived on a river and loved canoeing. His father once used the river as an analogy about life that he said always stuck with him. He said, "A river is forward moving. There's no chance of stopping it. Some rocks and rough patches. Occasionally you might get stuck in the tall reeds where you can't see what is in front of you—until the current finds you again. And the current *always* finds you again. Then away you go. Growing and learning—and becoming more from *all* of it—until you merge back into the ocean."

Gabe's father also obviously knew his way around the Bible. His job was to teach historical context and hermeneutics to undergraduates. But his father taught him that the Bible has been misused. He said that we forgot that there are sixty-six *very* different books in there. Seventy-three in the Catholic Bible. Each one unique—and should be treated as such. He believed that it contains only snippets of the story of our human origins and much of that is symbolic and metaphorical. And he taught Gabe that he believed that *God* did not change from the Old Testament God to the New Testament God. He didn't believe that there was *ever* an angry, damning God. But he said that we—*we*—are the ones who have changed ... and are changing. And he said that ancient people had *always* told stories of controlling and angry gods in the sky. He said that he believed that the stories in the Old Testament were just people's attempts to explain—and make some kind of sense—of God from their very limited vantage point. And many of these stories had been passed down orally for thousands and thousands of years before ever being written in symbols and letters.

He told Gabe he ultimately believed that modern cultures don't know how to use the power of sacred, ancient scriptures and instead just try to beat each other over the head with them. Gabe laughed and said his father compared modern men reading ancient texts to "a cave man trying to do trigonometry." He said that the essence of ancient storytelling had been lost. He felt like this was a great tragedy and had hindered our spiritual progress as a society. Gabe's father said that we didn't know how to live within the beautiful mystery of it all and that so much love and meaning had been sacrificed on the altar of inerrancy and literal interpretation.

His father said ironically that one of the sources of the misunderstanding was the interpretation of "word" in the Bible. Gabe's father said that God's "word" was actually translated from the word 'logos" which has a much broader meaning than—these literal words in these books. He said that the logos is living and breathing and expanding. *Always* expanding. *Always* creating. It is the essence of God. And there are no human words that can capture the *logos* of God—the *essence* of God—the creative force behind galaxies.

His father taught him that as much as we want it to be, language has never been an exact science and there are spiritual concepts in the Bible that can't be put into any combination of letters or symbols—in any language. And he explained that some of the books of the Old Testament, like the Psalms, are almost living and breathing and can only be fully *experienced in* prayerful contemplation.

His father also taught him that our spiritual journey is a deeply individual one. And we are all on the same path—just different places on it. And this is one reason Jesus said not to judge. We can't see the entire map of a person's divine plan. And our time is best spent focusing on the beam in our *own* eye and our *own* next step in our personal journey.

And his father said—yes —he believed that Jesus had and has a unique mission here. And—yes—Jesus is divine. But that we are *all* made in God's image—we *all* have the potential to be the sons of God. And that Jesus came to demonstrate that path. He came here to demonstrate *the Way.* He said that we forget that Jesus had his own journey that he had to take while he was here. Heartache, rejection, betrayal ... the temptations in the wilderness ... the baptism in the Jordan ... the *giving up of his life* on the cross ... and finally his ascension. Gabe's father said that Jesus didn't want to start a new religion— certainly not one that persecuted others in his name. He didn't want us to worship him. He wanted us to *emulate* him.

I said, do you believe that?

"That he wants us to emulate him? Yes—of course, if not, why would he even teach all of the lessons? Why would he even bother?"

"No. I mean ... do you believe that we all have the potential to be the sons of God?

Gabe said, "It makes perfect sense to me. Did you not ever read where Jesus refers back to Psalms where it says, 'Ye are gods' ... maybe meaning, 'you are all sons, creators.'"

I kind of laughed and said, "Ye are gods? No. I never heard any sermons on that one. That's for sure."

Listening to Gabe, I felt like I needed to delete everything I *thought* I knew about God. I definitely wanted to revisit Psalms. And more of Jesus' teachings. And try to reread them with this different perspective. I thought, *maybe Jesus didn't choose the well-educated as his disciples for good reason.* He definitely didn't choose the haughty "religious" of his day. They were unteachable. Maybe this is why Jesus said that you have to be like a child to "enter the kingdom." Gabe said his father would always say, "Leave some room for wonder. Leave room for God to be the God of all the heavens and not just our tiny corner of it." I wish that I could have met Gabe's father. It was almost like Gabe grew up on a different planet.

***

The Nine Lives of Jezebel

Soon after, Gabe, Rebecca, and I met at my apartment; we ordered pizzas from this amazing place downtown. Hand-tossed. Huge slices. I made a big salad with thinly sliced red onion, cucumber and green pepper with a homemade Green Goddess dressing out of fresh avocado. Rebecca thought it was delicious. Gabe wouldn't touch the salad. I did have one victory. I had some banana peppers. I talked Gabe into squeezing them on his cheese pizza. He loved it but tried to pretend he didn't. I rubbed it in that he was having a vegetable. He said that pepper juice "hardly counted." Rebecca was all business. Gabe and I would get to talking or laughing about something, and she would get us right back on track. I did appreciate that about her. Sometimes, ocean dwellers need a good lifeguard around.

Everything was going well. Perfectly. But after we finished eating, I noticed Rebecca looking at a Buddha figurine on my mantle that I had bought at a thrift store with Flora. I wasn't attached to it. It meant very little to me beyond the aesthetics of it. But her eyes kept going to it. It was like I had left drug paraphernalia up there or something. And I had seen that look before. Too many times. I had this sudden urge to hide it—like I was doing something wrong. I was back in that church hallway being reprimanded by the pastor's wife.

I said, "Do you like my Buddha?" I almost wanted her to believe that it was my idol—my shrine.

"Well ... I wouldn't say that." She kind of rolled her eyes and said, "I knew you were one of those people."

"What kind of people would that be?"

"You know ... a New Ager."

"New Ager?" *What twenty-something even uses that term?* I laughed sarcastically. Suddenly, our egos materialized—right here on my couch. Full view. It was almost a relief. Finally, no more faking it.

"My God, Rebecca. Do you even know who Buddha was?"

"Of course I do."

Flora had taught me a few things I didn't know about Buddha when I bought it. Information that probably came from her mom. I said, as if I was some kind of expert, "Did you know that Buddha gave up riches to follow the spiritual path?" I didn't give her time to answer. I kept firing away. "Did you know that some believe that Buddha and Jesus actually taught a lot of the same things? Did you know that Buddha lived a whole five hundred years before Jesus? So, not so *New* Age huh, Becky?" She had mentioned that she hated being called "Becky." So, I did—of course. She didn't know any of it. She wasn't allowed to know any of it. I felt that old rage. In that moment, I had no grace for Rebecca. Not one ounce of it.

She rolled her eyes while getting her phone out of her purse and said, "Whatever you say, Laine. I'm a Christian. We just don't follow other religions. That's all. And by the way, I don't appreciate you using the Lord's name in vain. You do it all the time."

"Christian? Christ-like, Rebecca? Are you? You are *like* Christ? Ummkay. Well, that's a hefty claim. And Buddhism isn't a religion, Rebecca. Buddha was a spiritual teacher. And you know what? Christianity shouldn't be a religion either. If you read your Bible, you might know that Jesus railed against the 'religious' in his day." Gabe looked at me sternly. I continued anyway. "They are the ones that killed him because he didn't line up with *their* scriptures. Remember that part of your Bible? He didn't come to start another effed-up religion, Rebecca. And if so—I'm certain that it wasn't supposed to look like *your* brand of it. And as far as using the Lord's name in vain, you ... *you people* ... are the ones using the Lord's name in vain. You use it to hate. You use it to judge. You use it to sit high up there in your ivory towers looking down on everyone that doesn't believe exactly like *you* do." By that time, I was up and off the couch.

I had crossed the line. Gabe stopped me. He looked at me and said, "Unless any of this adds to the volunteer training, peace and love, but it's irrelevant right now." He probably regretted sharing any of his father's teachings with me. I had weaponized them.

Rebecca could have been any random girl in my Sunday school class back home. Her brand of Jesus had been the brand I was raised on not that long ago. Even with all the lessons, I had returned to the scene of the crime and failed. She was right. I was using the Lord's name in vain. We both were.

Some progress was made, I guess. At least I didn't beat myself up like I had after I ruined Christmas with Uncle Jeff. Just because I failed to show her grace doesn't mean I needed to fail to show it to myself. Like my counselor taught me, self-forgiveness is just as important. I had definitely learned that wallowing in your guilt and shame serves absolutely no purpose. And when you know better, you just get right back up and do better. Dammit. You just get up and do better. I didn't self-loathe this time, but I knew that I was done word vomiting on people. It was time that I released this grudge too. This baggage. It was time that I give Christianity the same grace I gave Dylan. The whole damn religion. All the way back. It wasn't even about Rebecca. She was just in my line of fire. And I hurt her. On purpose. There was no excuse.

Chapter 10

Songbird

Not long after that day, Gabe and I decided to eat our lunches at the picnic tables near this big Sugar Maple outside of the hospital. It had turned a marigold color. And there was a blanket of leaves on the ground around it. It was breathtaking. As we finished up, Gabe talked about how his father loved trees and could name every kind when they were out in the woods. He also taught him that trees are alive in the sense that they have a physiological reaction when a branch is cut. And the trees around it have a measurable reaction if the tree is cut down. I told him I had read something similar.

We sat back and looked at the tree in silence. Some branches getting weaker with fewer leaves. Some branches strong, brand new. Others completely lifeless and ready to fall.

Gabe smiled and said, "The planet is just a big, beautiful Sugar Maple, Lainey. That's all. Some branches falling away. Some just sprouting. But we are all of the same tree. All of us. If you hurt one branch, we all get hurt."

Our eyes met. I knew exactly what he was saying. Rebecca. I nodded my head slowly. "Yes." I had nothing to say for myself.

Gabe adored the babies. We would both go to the nursery sometimes just to coo and stare. I can't remember why I was up there. But one day, I saw him from a distance looking in the window at them. The hallway was dark. His hands were resting in his jacket pockets. I suddenly felt sad for him standing there all alone. I realized that with his health issues, he might not ever have children of his own. I quietly snuck up next to him. I didn't speak at first. There was a brand new baby boy right next to the window who was awake. He wasn't crying—he was alert—looking around. Just a swaddle with big, dark blue eyes. Almost looked extraterrestrial. Gabe and I were both captivated. It was his first hours out of his safe cocoon. So new. I suddenly had mixed feelings—knowing how hard this world can be, but at the very same time, knowing this little guy had his whole life ahead of him. He had made no mistakes yet.

Gabe finally broke the silence. He said, "So brave."

I said, "Yeah ... he has no idea about mean girls, acne, school, cafeteria food. Let's not tell him. Okay?"

Gabe smiled. Then he said, "Oh he knows all of it. But he still chose to come." There were a few moments of silence. Then he said, "Planet Earth can be a tough school. One of the toughest. Only the bravest volunteer. And the very bravest are the ones who choose a hard path. They come knowing they'll be persecuted or shunned. It's a mission of pure love. People don't realize it, but those who we see as disadvantaged are our most noble teachers in disguise." It wasn't like Gabe was wondering. It was like he was *remembering*.

About that time, a nurse came in to take the baby back to his mother. We walked down the hall to the elevator in silence.

I finally said, "Are you hungry?" We decided some croissants were in order. By the time we got back to our offices, he was back to his happy self and whistling again.

I said, "What is it you are whistling?" I recognized it, but I could never figure it out.

He whistled a line of Taylor Swift's "I Knew You Were Trouble."

"Not that one, you jerk." He always said jokingly that he "knew I was 'trouble when 'he' walked in."

He said, "Okay let's see ... this one?" He whistled it again.

"Yeah ... that's your go-to, it seems. I can't put my finger on it."

Then, he stopped. He said, "'His Eye Is on The Sparrow' You know ... the old gospel hymn."

My whole being smiled. He whistled it all the way back into his office.

Gram used to say, "God speaks to us all of the time. We just have to pay attention."

Chapter 11

Love Stories

By the end of October, we were pretty much ready for the training. And the tension between Rebecca and I eased a lot after I mustered up an apology. I was behaving. Gabe asked us both to help him look for near-death experiences that were particularly uplifting to share with the volunteers. One of his goals was to lessen their personal fear of death. This ended up being life-changing for me. I was guessing he knew that.

We were going into a rainy and cold weekend. I had a paper to finish for school. But I had been wanting a good book. I decided I would go to the community library and see what they had on NDEs. I love holding a real book in my hands. They actually had several. I grabbed two. They were both older books. One was written by a woman who died in her late twenties with young children. The other was a man who died an atheist but ended up going to seminary after his experience. I decided that I would read the mother's story on Saturday and the other story on Sunday.

I stopped by the grocery on Friday night, and I chatted with Mom and Dad on the phone while I shopped for some comfort foods and a new kind of hot tea to try. They had a food bar that I loved there. I got a big container of white chili. A jar of jalapeño peppers. I also got a loaf of sourdough bread that was still warm in the bag. I splurged on some Gouda cheese and fresh sesame crackers that they also made in the bakery there. I found some giant red seedless grapes and some Hibiscus and Tulsi tea.

Oh. I almost forgot to tell you about the call.

That night, I had a bowl of my chili while I finished up my paper for school. My phone buzzed. And my heart stopped. It was Dylan. I never imagined that I would ever hear from him again. I started to answer. Then, I laid my phone down, held my breath and just stared at his name across the screen. How that sight used to make me so happy. I rarely thought about Dylan anymore. I was in such a better place. Finally, the phone was silent. I looked to see if he left a voicemail. Nothing. Now, I'm not going to lie. There was a part of me that wanted to answer the call. There was this part of me that wanted to hear him tell me I'm beautiful again and hang on every word I said as he weaseled his way back into my life. Even if he didn't mean a word of it.

Being "wanted" feels so good. I had never felt so "wanted." But I will tell you what feels a million and a half times better—being respected. Just good old-fashioned respect. I found out that it's way more satisfying. And it has a way longer shelf life. So, I just sat there. *Maybe he had just been in town and ran out of gas? Maybe he wanted the name of a restaurant we ate at one time? Maybe he wanted to apologize. Or maybe he just butt dialed me.* It didn't matter.

I had just returned to the scene of that particular crime and passed that test with flying colors.

Saturday morning, I toasted a slice of my sour dough. I treated myself with generous amounts of butter and strawberry jam that my mom and Aunt Patricia made. I made a cup of the Tulsi tea. And as my tea cooled, I picked up the book written by the young mom. I looked at the cover. There was a picture of her on the back. She looked pretty normal. Strawberry blonde hair. Attractive. I had never met anyone that had an NDE. I was kind of surprised that I had never really had any interest in reading about them. It was such an ocean-dweller kind of thing to do. And Gabe was telling us that they are becoming more common and more talked about. He said that, interestingly enough, a lot of doctors and scientists were reporting having them personally. Of course, that got my attention. Those two worlds colliding.

I dove right into it. It was a small book. I could easily finish it in one day. I thought I might read a couple of hours before taking a break. But that didn't happen. There were no breaks. I literally couldn't put it down. It traveled with me to the bathroom—to the kitchen that afternoon where I barely could slap a sandwich together without stopping—back to the bathroom—back for two more mugs of tea—and back to the couch where I planted myself and finished it before dinner. When I was done, I just sat there. And I realized, without a doubt, that there was a definitive before and after this tiny book. It may have been one of the most pivotal moments in my God story so far, and there was no going back from it. It felt almost divinely placed in my hands.

Her story was terrifying and beautiful. But it was confirmation of everything I had always felt in my soul to be true. I had been starving for that my whole life. Proof. Confirmation that there was no mean grandfather God with a long beard on a throne just chomping at the bit to judge our souls and damn us to hell. There was so much love. Love, love, and more love. Not conditional love. Not unpredictable love. *Perfect* love.

There were so many details about her story that struck me. But the one thing that probably struck me the most was that even though her entire life was completely devoted to her family, she struggled with the decision to go back to them. In that dimension, she clearly understood that they were souls—part of her but also separate from her—on their *own* journey. And that their souls would always be bound in love. She would be with them in a sense. But it was okay if she chose not to return to her body here on Earth. Her children's lives would play out, and they would have good times, bad times, lessons of their own. And they would have lessons from the experience of losing her too—if she chose to stay.

The idea of it was unimaginable. We are so attached to our people. I thought about my grandmother in that hospital room. Maybe this is why I intuitively felt like she had just arrived back home. It was her *real* home.

The next morning, I thought about the second book as soon as my eyes opened. I jumped right out of bed. I made a cup of Hibiscus tea. I studied the cover. It was different. And the title was a bit shocking. I have to admit that I was a little guarded as I opened it. But I vowed to stay open to whatever message it delivered.

The author of the first book was loving. This guy was not. He admitted it. He didn't like people in general. He drank too much. He was a miserable person. He died fairly young too—late thirties. And he died a devout and proud atheist. His death also came suddenly. And he found himself almost immediately in a hellish experience. He had no golden ticket. I was as captivated by this story as I was the first one. Maybe more so. *This was it*. This guy was experiencing everything that my denomination preached. Hellfire and damnation. But here was the game changer—he didn't stay there. I guess he could have. But as soon as he called out for God, the light scooped him right up. He felt all the love—all of it—as though he had never been separated from it. And he got to have some very intense conversations with this omniscient intelligence he recognized as Jesus. In fact, after he returned and recovered, he dedicated his whole life to learning and teaching about him—as a minister.

I finished that book as quickly as I had finished the one the day before. When I was done, I went back and reread the part where the light met him in his hell. That was the missing piece. Like I suspected as a kid, grace doesn't run out. God, like any father worth their salt, *always* seeks reconciliation. We are all prodigal sons and daughters. How could we have ever thought it to be any different?

Over the next several days, I had a hard time focusing on school. Just one more story. *Just one.* There are tons of books about NDEs. Videos. Podcasts. People everywhere and all ages are having near-death experiences and even pre-birth experiences where they have knowledge of their souls before their current life or even previous lives. There are tons of documented cases—even children who remember past lives in incredible detail. I wondered, why aren't more people obsessed with these stories? I soon remembered why some aren't.

That Thursday, Gabe texted Rebecca and me to see if we could meet in his office one last time before the training. He wanted to make sure all the materials were in order and to get our thoughts on a few things. And he wanted to make a last-minute attempt to market the training in the lobby that weekend. He had twelve new volunteers sign up so far. His goal was fifteen. He also, of course, wanted to hear if we had found any stories that were especially interesting. I couldn't wait to talk about them with someone. Near-death experiences are not something you just chat about with your lab partner or the guy that sits behind you in statistics class. NDEs are not really great conversation starters on a college campus.

I basically took over our little meeting. I went on to tell them about this one and that one ... and oh, oh this one. All love stories. These people of all faiths, ages, life circumstances literally inundated with Divine Love and life-changing remembrance of who we really are—our souls. And I wanted to go to every room in the hospital and tell them too. All of them. I wanted to yell it from the rooftop. I finally felt free. I wanted to free everyone. And I wanted to free Rebecca. I saw her divinity. I saw all of our divinity. If we only knew. If we only could remember—it would change everything.

Rebecca sat patiently with her legs crossed and her hands tightly wrapped around her knees. I finally managed to stop talking. I looked at Gabe. He said, "Okay ... you can breathe now." We laughed. Rebecca didn't.

Then we both looked at Rebecca. I noticed she started shaking her leg nervously. I thought maybe she didn't look for any stories, and she was embarrassed. That would be totally out of character for her. She may have been the most responsible person I had ever met. Her color-coded planner was a literal work of art. We knew she hadn't forgotten.

Then, she finally spoke. She looked at Gabe, cleared her throat, and said, "I'm just going to be honest here, Gabe. I think that these stories are entertaining and all, but I feel like they have no place in our training." I watched Gabe's energy shift. It was like he was getting ready to cradle a baby.

His movements slow and deliberate, his voice lower and softer, he said, "Why do you think that, Rebecca?"

She replied, "They just aren't biblically sound, Gabe."

"How so?" He knew exactly what she meant. There was no mean grandfather type on his throne in the stories. There was no damning judgment. The "unsaved" were slipping through the cracks somehow.

She crossed her arms, "I read some of them. I'm sorry, but this is nothing but the work of Satan, guys. The Bible warns us against this stuff. False prophets. Other than Jesus, there were only two people who have ever seen God and lived ... Moses and you know ... that other guy ..." She struggled for a second to remember the name.

I said, "I think there were actually several. There was Jacob and —"

She interrupted me and said, "It doesn't matter. Nobody else has ever seen God or heaven and lived to talk about it—except them. These are all lies from the pits of hell—or hallucinations."

I took a deep breath. I was back at the scene of the crime. But I definitely knew better. *I will do better this time. So help me, God. I will do better.*

Gabe looked a little nervous as I took the floor again. I borrowed a tip from my counselor. I first "validated her feelings." I said, "Rebecca, I understand where you are coming from." I really did understand. Completely. Like I said, she could have been any girl in my Sunday school class. Just like for my Sunday school teachers there, it's like a house of cards. If you pull one card out, it all falls down. These stories challenged the whole construct of her safety net in life. This is absolutely terrifying to some people. This is why Gabe handled her so carefully and lovingly. Their whole sense of security in the world rides on every word of the Bible being literal. *Every word.*

And ironically "spiritual" things can be scary for some Christians. Even though the Bible is full of stories of angels and visitations —and all kinds of spiritual happenings. It's still suspect. We were taught about the archangels and the ascension and talking animals and a talking bush and Jesus even walking around—having a meal with his disciples in spirit form—after his crucifixion. What could be more *woo-woo* than that? But, well, that was Jesus, and all of that was "back then." One of the go-tos in my church was that the Devil would present himself as an angel of light when deceiving God's people. So, basically, you can't trust spiritual experiences unless they happened to people 2,000 years ago.

But I surprised myself. I calmly said, "Rebecca, you may not know this about me, but I grew up how you did. And for whatever reason, God put it in my heart a long time ago to question every part of what you and I were taught. I'm not going to apologize for that. I believe it was my path. It was the journey I had to take—and one I'm still taking. I guess I won't understand it until I have my own "death experience." But these stories validated what I felt in my heart to be true from the time I was a little girl. You are on your *own* journey, Rebecca. And you are exactly where you need to be on it. I honor that. I am exactly where I need to be. You should honor that too. And I feel like we should honor these volunteers by letting them be wherever they are on *their* path. These volunteers are adults. They can take from these stories whatever they need. And they can reject what they don't need. It is not our job to dictate that for them."

We were all silent for a second. I could feel Gabe's pride for his little Lainey. I waited for Rebecca's response. But as surprised as I was at my own composed extension of the olive branch, I was equally surprised at her response to it.

She saw it all quite differently. She shook her head, laughed sarcastically, and said, "Laine, you just need a good Bible study. A really good one. One that is firmly rooted in the word of God. We have one that meets every Wednesday night at church. Pastor Wayne teaches it himself. Well ... he's the associate pastor. He has a master's degree in theology. He knows the Bible from front to back. You are more than welcome there." She waited for my response with a look of pity.

I was tempted to tell Rebecca I had spent my whole life in Sunday school and Bible studies. And I was well aware of how it would go in her Bible studies too. Instead, I just said, "Thank you for the invitation."

It feels good to keep the promises you make to yourself. I'm learning it's a huge piece in having self-respect. You hear all the time about having healthy boundaries with other people. But nobody ever talks about having those boundaries with yourself. Like, I, Patricia Elaine Anderson, will not engage in arguments about God. I mean—really? Think about it. It's like arguing about the color orange. Or the scale and size of the universe. None of us even has the language for it. So many of the near-death experiencers I read about said, "I have no words. I just have no words." They had no man-made characters and symbols to put together that would adequately describe the infinite source of all of creation. I guess it's preposterous to think we would.

We got seventeen people signed up for the training. Exactly fifteen showed. Gabe used four very different near-death experiences. It was a complete success. We only used half of our budget. And Rebecca and I made it through without any more incidents. Gabe and I laughed afterwards when he, with his best announcer voice, said, "And we gladly report that no people were harmed in the making of this hospice training." It was a close call.

Chapter 12

Mind over Matter

Flora, James, and I had a "Friendsgiving" the night before we all were going home for Thanksgiving break. We didn't do much cooking. James picked up Thai food for old time's sake. We were in a pumpkin rotation and went with the traditional pumpkin pie for our dessert. Flora used a real pumpkin. No canned stuff. We roasted the seeds in the oven. I enthusiastically shared that pumpkin seeds, in fact, kill intestinal parasites if ground up into a fine powder. James said, "Well, you know I heard that Thai restaurant did get a C from the health department on cleanliness." James was always good for some snark. And I was always good for a fun food fact to nerd things up a little. But what I really couldn't wait to share with them was about the NDEs.

They were both open and equally as fascinated. James especially was, as it was relevant to the workings of the brain. We talked about how some of them might be initial reactions to anesthesia or trauma. He said he thought there may be some residual subconscious mixed in with some of the experiences. But he agreed there was just no possible way all of these people were having such similar experiences that resulted in a shift in their everyday reality afterwards and it be purely physiological. In fact, some had such a shift or a sense of homesickness afterwards that they suffered from clinical depression. Some left marriages or jobs. Some quit or changed churches. Some started going to a church for the very first time in their life.

Of course, it wasn't a matter of convincing James and Flora. They were deep divers. Long-time ocean dwellers. And although they didn't feel the need to advertise it, they also both had faith in something much bigger than themselves. They didn't obsess about the details like I did. They didn't need to apply their intellect to any mystical teachings. And they were more about the *doing* than the knowing. Maybe they already knew. Maybe they had already climbed Knowing Mountain. Maybe they had climbed it lifetimes before. And they were there just extending their hand to those—like me—who were clumsily trying to make their way up.

The next day, it was a long drive home for such a short visit, but I had lots to keep my mind busy. You can probably guess what podcasts I downloaded. It was my new passion—bordering obsession at that point. Similar threads ran through every story. Often a tunnel to a light ... almost always a life review ... beings of light ... or deceased relatives or pets that came to greet them. But even though I noticed the similarities, the differences also began to stand out. And they often correlated closely with the experiencer's life, beliefs, state of consciousness when they died. The state of their "kingdom within."

People who were committed to their Christian faith would often see Jesus. Of course, some who were not Christian also saw him. Some were welcomed by a grandparent, a friend, their angels, or other "wise beings."

I read one story of a scientist who had no belief in the afterlife at all. She had a beautiful life review. Her life was shown to her inside of these droplets of water that rippled out into larger circles. She could see the impact that her actions had on all of these people she had met. Meetings that seemed insignificant. Good and bad. And she got to feel what the other person was feeling and how it literally rippled out into how they, in turn, treated others. She was forever changed and speaks and writes about her story to this day. She wasn't burned in hell for her lack of belief. She was loved, instructed— and sent back to help us to remember the impact of our own ripples.

And these ripples can begin with our thoughts. In fact, one of the biggest eye-openers I got from the stories was the power of our thoughts. I was a bit shaken as one of the experiencers said he was told that it's not just our actions that have an impact on those around us. But our thoughts can literally damage someone on some level. Maybe that's another reason why Jesus taught not to judge—to pray for our enemies. He knew that we have that kind of power. Imagine if someone in your town is suffering with an addiction or has done something terrible, and every soul around them just pummels them with judgment and negativity. How much harder is it for them to pull themselves up? Maybe impossible. It's humbling and terrifying and amazing—all at the same time. But on the flip side, think about it. We can help bring healing to each other with our minds too. We can help lift each other out of our pits. Suddenly, "I'll pray for you" or sending "good vibes" are less cliché. Jesus said, "Truly I tell you, if you have faith as small as a mustard seed, you can say to this mountain, 'move from here to there,' and it will move. Nothing will be impossible for you." Jesus also said, "What I can do, you can do also." Like him, maybe we can also be the conduits for divine healing. And if two or more gather, it's amplified. One near-death experiencer said she could actually see prayers shooting up like flares of light from the planet.

Maybe we have forgotten that heartfelt prayer is our greatest superpower.

The other incredibly beautiful thing that struck me about these experiences was that the settings were so unique and seemed to be especially designed for the experiencer. It might be in a field or by a river. It might be in their grandmother's kitchen if that was where the soul felt the safest. It might be on the pew of a church. It might all take place in the cosmos. Every experience tailored to the experiencer. It's like God allows the soul to adjust to being back home. Whatever that soul needs.

And yes, absolutely. One hundred percent. Some people report having a hellish experience.

But maybe that hellish experience didn't start there. It just carried over from their hellish experience on Earth. Maybe you will be given what you need to move your soul along on its journey. And if that's a period of hell—which is essentially a separation from the light of God—yes, maybe you have the free will to experience that too. Like the experience of the second book I read, he was angry, mean, proud. Maybe his soul *needed* that terrifying experience. Without it, he would never have reached for the light.

Maybe your consciousness doesn't just turn off like a light switch. Maybe it's just amplified. Without your physical body, you are *only* consciousness. Pure consciousness. Everything is more vivid and real. Even our hells. But maybe you can change your consciousness at any time—*here* or *there*. It's just a matter of changing your perspective. Like changing the channel. Our minds are powerful instruments. And can be the conduits for all that is holy—or not. The law of free will held sacred.

And maybe there are an infinite number of heavens and hells. Frequencies. Jesus said, "There are many mansions." Our souls, without the physical body, are pure energy. And maybe they are drawn to similar frequencies. Positive and negative. And maybe we can anchor the frequency of heaven here if we bring it here—through our pure intentions. "Thy kingdom come. Thy will be done. On Earth as it is in heaven." Maybe Jesus the Christ "returning" is simply us remembering who we really are—and *us* anchoring the *spirit* of Christ here on Earth.

Think about it. Maybe salvation is not a one-way ticket to a better place. Maybe it's just a turning toward the light—wherever your soul is on its journey. Maybe access to the kingdom of God is right there within you. Always has been. Always will be.

Maybe Jesus' message was cheapened. The lessons—his deeper, mystical teachings—turned into this man-made ironclad doctrine that never made any sense to any of us—if we are *really* honest with ourselves. It's no wonder that so many people are turned off by it all. Maybe it's in direct conflict with our soul's *knowing*. Maybe that is the gift in these thousands and thousands of stories. Messages across the ethers. Maybe they are love notes from home. Maybe it's time. Maybe it's time that we all remember.

A person can definitely do a lot of thinking on an eleven-hour car ride.

***

The Calm

Ok. Back to Earth and my cozy bed at home. I got in late. We all just said our hellos and tiptoed off to bed. Gus had completely changed allegiances. After he said hello and got his scratch on the head, he bypassed my bedroom and snuggled up in Dad's chair. He was clearly my dad's cat now. I learned that my mom now referred to them as "her boys." So, basically, he had replaced me. I didn't mind.

We sometimes spend Thanksgiving with my Aunt Heather's family. It is the only time we see them all year. They are only about four hours away by car. They were coming to our house that year. Trips to see them were vivid childhood memories. On the way, we would stop and shop a little for Christmas. We always stopped and got her family some pecans and cashews at this place near the outlet mall. It was kind of like the kick-off of the holiday season. My dad's older sister, Heather, and her husband, Dan, had one son. He was in graduate school on the west coast. He wouldn't be home that year. So, they drove to see us. They got there sometime in the night. About the time that I was frolicking in the tall grass again.

All of these NDEs were making for some interesting dreams. Of course, my dreams are always interesting. But I rarely have one that I feel like has any significance. You know ... the basic naked-at-school dream or your-teeth-falling-out dream.

This dream was brief. I was a little girl. Tall green grass. It was beautiful. The dream had a different quality to it. And when I woke up at my parent's house, I had the time to really think about it before it left me. I don't know if you do this, but if I don't tell someone about it or write it down, it's gone by lunch. It's like my brain just deletes it. I tried to recall any unusual details. I think I was wearing a dress? Yeah ... I was definitely wearing a dress. I could feel it brushing up against my legs as I ran. I definitely wasn't scared. It was more than a lack of fear. It was more like joy. Sunshine and joy. I struggled to remember anything else. I had nothing.

Suddenly, this amazing aroma made its way back to my room. My parents had been up and drinking coffee with Heather and Dan. They had returned the favor this year and brought the cashews and pecans. Mom had roasted the pecans in brown sugar and cinnamon in the oven. The smell drew me straight into the kitchen. Talk about heaven. My mom was pulling them out of the oven. My aunt and uncle got up from their chairs. My Aunt Heather squeezed me and kissed me between my eyebrows just like she always did. She told me years ago that was the most sacred of kisses. Between the eyebrows. Her quirkiness was always endearing. I wondered if she knew about the struggles I had last year. I didn't care if she did. Like James and Flora, she is a *safe* person. You don't feel like you have to put on airs for Aunt Heather.

And I hadn't realized it until I was older, but Heather had more hard-won substance than I ever understood as a kid. My dad used to say I had her free spirit and his mother's mean streak. Heather never went to college but had a PhD in making big life "mistakes." She was terrible at choosing men. Dan was her third husband. And after husband number two, Heather went hog wild. She was still in her twenties. She was restless and had an insatiable case of wanderlust. We still don't know this to be fact, but my dad thinks she actually lived in her car for a while. We do know she traveled around the country. She took a few trips to Denmark. She almost moved there. My dad said she enjoyed partaking in all the "activities." I only recently knew what he meant.

My dad's mother was completely horrified. She tried to shame her back into submission. She sent Heather nasty letters. They were returned unopened. All the shaming didn't work. My Aunt Heather just kept doing her thing—loving life and everyone in it along the way. She never got angry with my Grandma Anderson—not that I heard about, at least. She never gave up on romantic love either. She had several rotten relationships after the two failed marriages. But she never closed her heart. There's a lot of strength in that, I have grown to believe. Keeping your heart open. And life rewarded her for it. Big time. Her life—and her marriage to Dan—was a dream. He surprised her last year with a month in Greece. One of her bucket list places. Whatever made her happy—made him happy. The hallmark of true love, maybe.

Those few days with Aunt Heather were exactly what I needed. She tried to teach me to knit. She taught me how to French press coffee. We made mulled wine. We built the first fire of the year. We cooked a huge feast. It was the traditional Thanksgiving meal. Mom showed me how to make easy homemade rolls. We made pumpkin and chocolate chip pecan pies, fresh green beans, honey-roasted carrots, butternut squash casserole, apple and sage stuffing, garlic-smashed red potatoes. Mom did most of the cooking. Uncle Dan was always in charge of carving the turkey.

I mostly let my mind rest. No school. No deep ocean dives into other dimensions or the meaning of life. Just family, love, rest and food.

My old friends invited me out for Mexican the night after Thanksgiving. I told them that I would see them at Christmas. I felt my soul urging me to just rest. I listened.

Chapter 13

Lily of the Valley

I got back to school, a light snow on the ground. Back to the grind. It looked like I was on track for straight A's for the semester. I was still undecided if I should pursue medical school. I hadn't talked to my parents about how I would fund it. It was doubtful that they could even help me. And I needed to take the entrance exam. I didn't feel a big passion for it, not the passion that I should for such an undertaking. I guess sometimes, you don't know your path until it opens up right in front of you. And if someone showed it to you a minute sooner than it was revealed, you wouldn't believe them.

At the hospital, we were getting ready for the Christmas toy drive. It was one of the biggest events we did all year. I was busy with that. Gabe was back to his normal routine. He was doing more patient visits than when he was prepping for the training. In fact, he kept talking about one of them in particular. Lily. She was an elderly patient. She had been in hospice for longer than six months. That was what qualifies a patient for hospice—a six-month prognosis. So, he had spent a lot of time with her. She had one daughter. But she and the patient had a very strained relationship. Gabe told me she had just come back into her mom's life because she found out she was terminally ill. But they never really discussed what had happened. Lily's pain was being managed as best they could. She was barely eating. Of course, their goal was comfort.

Gabe was preoccupied with her situation. He was always very careful to protect patient confidentiality. But one day, he confided in me. He said, "Laine, she just won't let go. She's terrified. It's so hard to watch." I thought about all of the beautiful NDEs. I said, "Where do you think that fear comes from? Was she a fearful person when she was younger? Did she grow up in a hell-obsessed church like mine?" I mean ... some fear was completely natural and understandable. We are talking about death here. But what he was describing was actually out of the norm for most hospice patients. It's hard to imagine when you are in the throes of youth, but Gabe taught me that many people are naturally ready when the time comes.

Out of the blue, he said, "Could you go visit her? You've technically had the volunteer training. I will just log it as volunteer hours." We didn't talk about what I would do or say. I decided I would just do what felt natural. But this felt important to Gabe. "Of course I will go."

The next week, it actually worked out nicely because I was out in the community setting up donation boxes for the toys. I decided to get a bouquet of flowers for her. She was in the inpatient hospice. Room forty-seven—almost all the way at the end of a wing. It was quiet and kind of dark back there ... just the beeping of a machine down the hall. She was still coherent enough to respond. I introduced myself as someone who worked with her nurses. I mentioned Gabe for credibility. She perked up a little at his name.

I wasn't sure what to do. So, I took the bouquet of flowers and held them close to her. We examined each flower together. The perfection. The uniqueness. The beauty. She tried to raise her head to smell them. I said, "Isn't it amazing. We were given these just for our pleasure. I mean ... we can't even eat them. Well, most of them anyway." I laughed. She didn't. I was trying too hard. But I was going with it. I said, "Have you ever thought about that? Isn't that amazing, Lily?" She looked at me and gave me a faint, "Yes." But I could see the fear in her eyes. I studied her face. It was worn with time but still so beautiful. It was almost regal. I could tell that our short visit wore her out. As I placed the vase of flowers in her sight, she closed her eyes and drifted off to sleep.

Several days passed. I decided to go back and see her. This time I took some hand lotion. It was one of my favorites. Lavender. I always had some in my purse. I took the unopened tube out of the bag. She seemed to be sleeping. The rustling of the paper woke her. But she lit up when she saw me. I took her flowers to the sink to refresh the water. We marveled at them again. I pointed out that the pink rose right in the middle had really put on a show. It had bloomed completely out and was absolute perfection. She nodded her head in agreement.

I finally put the flowers away. I told her that I had brought her some lotion. I held the tube to her nose. She nodded enough for me to know she liked it. I asked her if I could put some on for her. I took a small amount and very gently rubbed it into her small, pale hands. I took a smaller amount and rubbed it into her cheeks and forehead. I smoothed her white hair with the tiny bit left on my hands. She seemed pleased. I said, "Doesn't that smell so good?" Barely moving her head ... I got a "yes" ... and a slight smile. She seemed a little more relaxed than last visit. I said, "I love all of the beautiful oils. Lavender, rose, clary sage, patchouli, frankincense, and myrrh. Some are believed to be healing, you know, and some just smell good. Made for no other purpose than our enjoyment, I guess." She nodded. I made sure my visits were brief. I never saw her daughter or any other family. Or any sign of them being there.

The hospice was close to campus. I started visiting Lily almost daily. I enjoyed it as much as she seemed to somehow. I took her a strawberry milkshake one day. The nurse said it was fine. She barely got any down, but we talked—or I did—about our favorite fruits and how they were made just for us. Our cells, like a lock and a key. I was probably just talking to hear myself at that point. It was basically the Intro to Nutrition right there in a dying patient's room. I know. Ridiculous.

But I think that what I really wanted to say to her and couldn't was "God's got you, Lily. He/She ... our Creator ... the Source of all that is and ever was isn't going to give us all of these perfect foods, gifts, experiences just for the simple sake of our pleasure, well-being, and joy just to drop us when that cord to this place is severed. I wanted to tell her that the beauty where she would be going is that rose in the center of her bouquet times a hundred bazillion. I wanted to say Lily, can't you see? You are going home! You are going home! We don't die, Lily. You are just going back to where you came from. But she had forgotten about home—just like we all had.

As finals were coming up, my visits became farther apart and briefer. At one point, I asked Gabe if I could put a bird feeder outside of her room. He got it approved. And he actually put the shepherd's hook in the ground and filled it with seed for me. I came and was thrilled that the birds had already discovered it. I moved the head of her bed up so she could see out the window. Tiny finches, cardinals, bluebirds. She seemed to love them the most, the bluebirds. For once, I felt no need to speak. We just sat in silence and marveled together.

As I was leaving one day, one of the nurses stopped me and said, "She is so much calmer since you've been visiting. Her daughter visits, but she is anxious after she leaves." I had to pretend that I didn't know about the conflict between Lily and her daughter. I certainly didn't want to take her place. I was just glad that I could be there to "help walk her home"... as Gabe called it. *It felt like the holiest of work.*

Christmas break was getting closer. I was studying for finals. At work, the toy drive kept me busy. Gabe and I tried to make time to catch up. He joined James, Flora, and myself for dinner one night. But Gabe and I were definitely due a lunch. I didn't like the distance growing between us. I missed him. I remembered when Flora moved home, and I lost my balance. I so desperately wanted things to stay the same forever. Ocean dwellers often do that, I think. We find our people, and we hold on for dear life. An ocean can sometimes feel like a treacherous place alone.

Chapter 14

I had a to-do list a mile long. Two more finals. I needed to wrap some things up for work. Clean my apartment. A few more gifts. And I wanted to see Lily one more time before going home for break. I was always aware that it might be my last. I stopped in the grocery store for some cleaning supplies and walked past the floral department. There were the most beautiful Stargazer Lilies. Like you normally only see at Easter. Just one bunch. *Lilies for Lily, how perfect*, I thought. I did a self-checkout and decided I would go straight there before home. I was kind of in a hurry. *I won't stay long.* They knew me at the nurse's station. So, I didn't do my usual check-ins, and I went straight back to her room.

As I approached her door, I slowed down. Something felt off before I even reached it. I walked in—the room was empty. The sheets were stripped from the blue plastic mattress. Only the light from the bathroom was still on. *Lily was home.* I could feel it. Her withering flowers had been removed from the windowsill. I put the fresh lilies on the bed, kissed my hand, closed my eyes, and touched the place where her body once lay. Any prayer or words felt inadequate for what had just taken place in that room.

As I was leaving, I saw the nurse I often spoke to, but she was on the phone. I decided not to disturb her. But as I pushed the doors open and a gush of cold air rushed in, I heard the nurse say as clear as a bell, "Dr. Anderson." My last name got my attention. But the "doctor" got the attention of my soul. I turned around before I even had time to process it. There she stood with her head down still talking on the phone. I sat in my car for a second. It was my sign that I prayed for in that hospital chapel. I was sure of it. More sure than I had been about anything in my life. I needed to start looking at medical schools.

I called Gabe. No answer. He never answered his phone. I thought, *I'll talk to him at work on Thursday. I'm sure he already knows.*

He will never leave me nor yet
forsake me here,
While I live by faith and do His blessed will;
It's a wall of fire about me, but
I've nothing now to fear,

With His manna He my hungry soul
is gonna fill.
Then I'll go sweeping up to Glory to see
His blessed face,
Where rivers of delight shall ever roll.
He's the lily of the valley, He's the
bright and morning star,
He's the fairest of ten thousand to my soul.
~ William Charles Fry

***

Fields of Gold

I felt pretty confident about my two finals I had to take the next day. You know that point where you are almost oversaturated with information, and any more just feels like it will do more damage than good. I set out to give my apartment a good scrubbing. I always clean to movie scores. I put on *Star Wars*. It's perfect for cleaning. I feel like I am saving the galaxy from the dirt and grime. It was after midnight when I finally got my shower and crawled into bed.

Early that next morning, I had the dream again. It woke me up. And I wasn't alone in this one. The field was different too. The sun was lower—like a fall feeling.

It was just as joyful. But I wasn't running in this one. I was walking toward this big tree with golden leaves. And under the tree was a boy. I was almost to him when I woke up.

I hit the snooze no less than five times the next morning. I made myself a big mug of strong coffee, grabbed a granola bar and banana, and I went to take my last finals. I had a break between those classes. Still refusing to open another book, I decided to go up to my spot in the library and just sit. As I was wrestling with my granola bar wrapping, I caught a fluttering out of the corner of my eye.

That night, I got the last of my gifts. I was at the point that I would wrap anything up. I thought, *Why is a poor college student buying rich people presents?* I got my Uncle Jeff a black scarf. I mean ... really? *Here is your $9.99 black scarf that you don't need and I bought with money that I don't really have. Wow. Thanks, Laine. I've always wanted a black scarf.* Ugghh. I get a little more bitter every year.

Gabe and I had this conversation about Christmas and giving. I didn't know his financial status. I knew he wasn't getting rich as the volunteer coordinator. But we talked about how much better it would be if for Christmas everybody went out—spent the same amount of money to keep the economy strong—but instead of buying crap for people who don't need more crap, just help someone. Can you imagine the joy? I mean ... honestly, going into the big box stores a few days before Christmas is enough to make a person want to quit the holiday altogether. Sad eyes. Long faces. Desperate young parents. The stress is palpable. They can barely buy groceries. And they are just trying to find something to put under that tree so that their kid doesn't think that Santa hates them. I bought a few things for the toy drive. Gabe and I were going to go in together and sponsor a whole family for Christmas. But we both had been so busy. We had barely seen each other. And honestly, I wasn't really in the position. I guessed he wasn't either.

With my apartment clean and my finals done, all I had left to do was finish packing the car for home. And with the toy drive almost over, I didn't have much going on at work the next day. I tidied up my office. I wondered what time Gabe was coming in to work. We had vowed we wouldn't do gifts for each other, but I wanted to do something.

I went to the hospital's gift shop. They had barrels of candy you could put in these little white bags. You paid by the weight. When we had gone up there before, he always just got the gross caramel ones with the marshmallow. I would gag and tease him for liking them. So, I filled a bag with those. And I looked for a Christmas card. I looked at every one they had. None of them jumped out at me. And if I liked the front, it would say something I didn't like inside. *I mean ... who writes this stuff anyway?* Then, I found the one. Only one of them left. There was a beautiful angel with a trumpet on the front. The colors were muted reds, blues, and gold. A gold lined envelope. It was simple. There was no message inside. I would write my own.

I got up to the register. The cashier weighed the candy. She took my card to scan. She kind of lit up.

"Ohhhh, I love this one. It's so beautiful."

"I love it too."

"It's Gabriel."

I just kind of nodded like I knew what she was talking about.

She said, "Archangel Gabriel. He's my favorite archangel."

On the elevator back down to the office, I searched Archangel Gabriel on my phone. *How perfect is this?* I couldn't wait to tease Gabe. "Archangel Gabriel."

I got back down to the office. I opened the blank card to write something. I can write forty bazillion research papers in a semester with almost no effort. And I couldn't find a string of a few words to write in a greeting card. I've always been this way. I guess it's how I was raised. Like I said, the Andersons are not doting people. I finally just started. I wrote on the envelope ... *My Dearest Gabriel.* He would get a kick out of that. Then I made my best attempt at sharing what was in my heart.

Gabe,

I have learned so much from you. And I have learned even more from watching you. You are such a bright light in this sometimes crappy, dark world. These patients are so lucky to have you. I'm even luckier to have you and call you my friend.

Merry Christmas!!

I love you,
Lainey

I sealed it up and set it on the corner of my desk. I set the bag of candy on top. I waited on him to eat my lunch. But lunchtime passed. I texted him. "Where are you?"

***

Broken Bones

I finished lunch. Gabe hadn't returned my text. He was terrible about it. The worst. But he hadn't been in all day. That was kind of unusual. And he hadn't returned my texts about Lily.

I was coming back from the bathroom when I saw Rebecca waiting on me at my door. She was just staring at me. Her arms folded. I could see a tissue clenched in one of her hands. She was wearing a heavy coat, yet she seemed to be shivering. As I approached her, she didn't speak. Her eyes were glossy. It was like she was searching my face for a sign. I guess she didn't find it.

She just said, "You don't know. Do you?"

I unlocked my office and asked her to come in and talk to me about it. *Had she been fired? Was she pregnant? Had she been diagnosed with some deadly, rare disease?* She just said, "It's Gabe" and surrendered to deep, long, inconsolable sobs.

There are stages of processing life-changing news, I think. Maybe it's designed that way. Like when you break your arm. It doesn't hurt at first. Then the throbbing sets in—gradually. It was like that. I had to first deal with Rebecca. She was almost hyperventilating right there in my office. I got up from my desk and just sat with her. I had no words for her—for either of us. She finally calmed down enough to give me some vague details.

Apparently, the Director of Hospice had called the staff in around eleven that morning. Gabe hadn't shown up for work the day before. They couldn't reach him. Then, when he didn't report that day either, they sent the police. It appeared he had died in his sleep. They were doing an autopsy. The whole team was dismissed to go home.

Rebecca finally pulled herself together. We sat in silence for a minute. I just stared at the bag of candy sitting there at the corner of my desk. And the card. *My Dearest Gabriel.*

It was starting to set in ... the throbbing part.

I honestly don't remember driving home or getting into my apartment. But when I did, I just went straight to my couch. I sat there with my coat still on ... and the throbbing turned into a deep ache. My arm wasn't just broken. It had been completely severed.

The truth is ... I don't care how many love stories about heaven a person reads, you just want your person back. That's all.

You just want them back.

Suddenly, I was looking for pieces of him. Evidence that he even existed. I remembered that he left a hoodie at my apartment. It had been hanging by the door for weeks. I got it and held it to my face as I scrolled through months of messages on my phone. Stupid memes. Lots of me fussing at him for not texting back. Lots of reminders to pick up something from upstairs in the hospital. Plans for lunch. Random meaningless things only a few hours ago—that meant the world to me now. I need just one more message. One more. But I knew one wouldn't be enough. Tens of thousands wouldn't be enough. I would have to go straight through this grief. Life was leaving me no choice this time. The unchangeable, immovable reality set in. He was gone.

My last message ... "Where are you?" Seriously ... I thought ...*Where are you?*

The next day, when I should have been about four hours into my trip home, I had to make the call. My mom answered. I tried to put up a strong front. I decided to go straight into it.

I said, "Hi Mom." I didn't give her time to talk. "Hey ... ummm ... there's been a change of plans. Well, do you remember me talking about Gabe?"

She cheerfully said, "Yeah, your friend at work. You said he didn't have any family. Is he coming home with you? You know that's totally fine. I'll get the guest bed ready. I just need to move some things off of it."

How did she even jump to that conclusion? I snapped back, "No. Mom. He's dead." I repeated, "dead." The bluntness of the word coming out of my mouth shocked me.

"Oh, Laine, Oh my gosh. I'm so sorry. So sorry. I know you will miss him so much. What happened ..." And then she said, "Hold on, Laine. I'm getting a call from the pharmacy. I need to take this. It will just take a second."

Really? Her casual approach to the whole thing made me livid for some reason. Suddenly, it wasn't so hard to tell her I was not coming home for break. In fact, it was easy. No grace for her. She should have known better.

But how could she have known what he meant to me? She had no idea. I didn't even really know until then.

I suddenly remembered my Gram saying, "When you feel like your world is caving in, just make your tea and bed." What choice do we have?

So, I did just that. I unpacked what I had put in my suitcase, started a list for the grocery store, and I texted Rebecca to see if she knew anything about the funeral arrangements. I didn't even know who would plan a funeral. Gabe had no living family. None that I was aware of anyway.

It was hours before she responded. I imagined that she was probably just trying to put one foot in front of the other like I was—probably busying herself too. But instead of texting me back, she called me. And she wasn't putting one foot in front of the other. She was hardly standing on her own two feet. I could barely understand her. Long sobs between incoherent strings of words. I hesitantly just asked her to come over. I told her that we would just go through this together.

Well, let's just say she took me quite literally. Rebecca showed up at my apartment that afternoon with an overnight bag and matching makeup bag. She was wearing her best athleisure. Her hair pulled back neatly. I casually asked her how long she could stay—like I even knew she had planned to in the first place. She said she had brought things just in case. Our Rebecca. Always prepared. My apartment had two bedrooms, but the second one had no bed. We would figure all of that out.

First things first. I had nothing in the fridge. I told her we needed to finish making a list for the store. She put her things in the second bedroom and plopped down on my couch with a tissue tightly gripped in her hand. I looked for a pen. She glanced up at my Buddha figurine and quickly looked away. I asked her if she had heard anything about the arrangements. She hadn't. I asked her what she might like for dinner. She "didn't care." I asked her if she was feeling better. She said "Yes." *Okay ... this is awkward.* I started making the list of things I knew I needed: sea salt, butter, cranberry juice, mandarin oranges. "How about pasta tonight? Sandwiches? Black bean tacos?" Everything I mentioned ... "Fine ... that's fine ... I don't really have an appetite."

I didn't either. I was just making my tea and bed.

As we were getting our coats, she got a text. It was her supervisor. She said Gabe's attorney was trying to pull together the arrangements and asked if staff would like to help. He had already contacted the chaplain. He was going to help if he could, but his wife was due with their first baby any minute. And if you needed something done, she probably knew Rebecca was your girl. Rebecca called her immediately. She began to tear up again. And her tears turned into those long, ugly sobs. Her shoulders violently shaking. She handed me the phone.

I had no clue who I was talking to on the other end. But I introduced myself to her. I told her I was also a good friend of Gabe's, and I worked in the marketing department at the hospital. She asked if I would like to help. I said, "Of course ... yes ... anything I can do."

We had more than a grocery list to plan now. We had to memorialize Gabe. His life needed to be celebrated. She gave me the attorney's name and number.

I had never been a part of planning a funeral. *Where do you even start?* Rebecca and I decided we would just talk to the attorney and let him guide us. He must have done this for clients before. She called and left him a message. We decided to just go out for dinner. Neither of us had an appetite. And we were too spent for grocery shopping. At dinner, the attorney, Jacob Bell, called her back. She pushed her plate aside. The tears started coming again. And soon, she was sobbing. She handed the phone to me. "Hi, Jacob." We planned to meet at his office the next morning.

Rebecca slept in my bed. I demanded it. I slept on the couch. She was anxious that she had nothing nice to wear to the appointment. We agreed we would both go to the appointment grungy. Of course, her version of "grungy" was much different than mine. We followed the GPS to the office. It took us to a high-rise downtown. I didn't know if Rebecca was thinking it too. *Why did Gabe need an attorney—one in a fancy high rise office?* When we got into the lobby, I was also suddenly anxious about how I was dressed.

We took the elevator to the eighth floor. I thought about the library. How many times I had pressed that eight. There were heavy glass doors right when you stepped off the elevator. There was an attractive young receptionist sitting there. Rebecca and I simultaneously looked down at our clothes and started to laugh. And you know how when you are in a situation where it is completely inappropriate to be laughing, and it makes you laugh even harder? It was like that. By the time we made it to her desk and she turned from her computer screen, we were crying laughing. Both of us. Here we were dressed like we just rolled out of bed. Well, I was anyway. And here we are in this fancy attorney's office to talk about a funeral—while laughing hysterically. There was so much wrong with all of it. Part of it was mental exhaustion, I'm sure.

The receptionist smiled at first. Then, she was clearly becoming irritated. When we were just about to pull ourselves together and tell her why we were there, a young guy in a suit, tie, and shiny wingtip shoes stepped out of the back hallway. He motioned us back. As I wiped the tears from my eyes, we followed him back to his office.

Jacob Bell appeared to be barely out of law school. He was basketball-player inches tall with dark hair and eyes. Rebecca shot me a look and raised her eyebrows. I quickly shut that down. We were not here to find a guy—and absolutely could not start laughing again. *This is serious. And I'm a little concerned. Has he ever handled an estate? I need to see his credentials.* In fact, I did start looking for them as he gathered a few things for our meeting and took a quick phone call. I scanned his bookshelves. Lots of legal books, of course. A couple of photos. But my eyes stopped on a stack of books almost set apart from the others. Rumi, Lao Tzu, C.S. Lewis, Eckhart Tolle—*no way*—Thomas Merton, Richard Rohr. *You've got to be kidding me.* I remembered Gabe talking about Richard Rohr. *Gabe probably gave him the book.* And sitting right on top of the stack was The Tao of Pooh. *The Tao of Pooh? This guy? There's no way.* I wondered for a second where my copy even went. And I thought, *Guys that work in high-*

rises with wing tip shoes don't read this stuff. Probably just decoration.

He wrapped up his phone call, and we finally got down to the business of why we were there. Gabe had chosen cremation in his will. We decided to wait until after Christmas to have the service. Jacob asked where we thought the service should be held. I remembered that Gabe said he grew up in an Episcopal Church. We decided the old Episcopal Church downtown would be perfect. It was built in the late 1800's. Beautiful, majestic, stained-glass windows. I had never been inside, but I would be in charge of contacting them.

He asked if we knew of anyone who might want to do the eulogy. I said I was sure the hospice chaplain would if he was able. Then, I surprised myself. I was terrified to speak in front of a church full of people. But I owed it to Gabe. I volunteered to speak as well.

We talked about music. Rebecca knew a violinist. I would talk to the pianist at the church. I said I would ask them for suggestions for music. Then I said, "Oh. I wonder if they can play an old hymn that was special to me." Jacob looked at me and said, "Which one is that?"

It suddenly hit me right there in Jacob Bell's office. *He's really never coming back. I'm never going to hear him whistling down that hallway again. This is really happening. Oh my God. This is really happening.* I suddenly couldn't get another word out. They were stuck in my throat. Rebecca put her hand on my back. Jacob looked at me with pain in his eyes and then down at his hands folded in front of him as if to give me privacy. Rebecca pulled a package of tissues from her purse, and after several minutes of failed attempts at words, we finally slowly moved on to talk about a wake at the church afterwards.

Rebecca said she would coordinate all the food. She kept repeating, "All of it. Nobody has to worry about any of that." She said the whole staff would want to help. She would reach out to them. "All of them." I fully realized her attempt to be brave in that moment. I grabbed her hand. Then, Jacob asked if we wanted to do the announcement about the gift in the service or wait until after when there might be an addition or something that would be dedicated to Gabe. Rebecca and I looked at each other.

I said, "What do you mean ... gift?"

He said, "Well. He left everything to the hospice. Some will be allocated to a scholarship in his mother's name. But most will be used however the hospice sees fit."

"Everything?" Rebecca said.

That was when we learned that Gabe had millions of dollars left to him.

I said, "Maybe it's none of my business, but where did he get all of this ... this money?"

Jacob seemed surprised. "He never told you about his mom?"

"Well ... yeah ... I mean ... he talked about her."

He explained, "She was quite a prolific artist. Her work was commissioned by some pretty famous people. And his parents lived a simple life really. They left Gabe everything. And as you probably know, he didn't spend much of it either."

Of course, Gabe would have never mentioned it. It wasn't his style. I thought about him in his khaki pants that needed hemming and that jacket he wore almost every day. Him digging around for a few coins for the drink machine. His brown bag lunches of white bread and bologna.

I was still processing all of it when Jacob looked at his watch. He had another appointment. We decided to communicate by email. So, he handed us both a business card and wished us a Merry Christmas. We waved to the receptionist on the way out. She forced a wave back.

Rebecca and I finally got back to my apartment. We both needed a nap. But more pressing ... lunch. I had nothing. We sat on the couch for a minute in awe of what we had just learned. We talked about if things would have been different if we all had known that Gabe was wealthy. Would we have acted differently around him? I was glad I didn't know. I wouldn't have changed a thing about my relationship with Gabe—except knowing him sooner.

I had texted James and Flora when I found out about Gabe's death. They had checked on me the night before. I got a text that they were bringing over some food. Relieved that we didn't have to go to the store after all, I wondered what Rebecca would think of them. They had never met.

Around five o'clock, James and Flora showed up at my door with a casserole dish and a bag of groceries. Flora had made a veggie lasagna. In the bags, there were two fresh baguettes, a bag of mixed salad greens, some brownies from the bakery, and a bottle of red wine. I thought about when Mom broke her arm last Christmas and the church was bringing food to us. It takes no building to be the church. James and Flora had always been the church to me. I begged James and Flora to stay. Rebecca got quiet around them at first. I noticed a few glances at Flora's clothes. I think she was wearing a sport coat. And maybe the green high tops. Her favorite. I can't remember. But it wasn't as awkward as I thought it would be. Pain is humbling. It quiets our egos.

We decided to put the lasagna back in the oven on warm and just relax for a bit.

I let Rebecca tell the story about Gabe's mom. And as she was finishing up, I heard a knock on my door. I opened it without a clue who would be standing there.

I literally jumped back. My dad. I tried to recover. "I mean ... oh my gosh ... I'm glad you are here ... but are you kidding me? You drove all that way?!" He smiled, "Santa sent me. AKA…your mom." And as I motioned him in out of the cold, my Uncle Jeff made his way to the top of the stairs with a breathless "Ho Ho Ho." He had several wrapped boxes. He handed them to my dad and told him he would be back up with the rest.

I took my dad's coat. He explained that they had gotten a room close by, but they just came to bring my gifts and to check on me. Jeff returned with a few more packages. I took his coat. I didn't have a tree, so I had them put the gifts in the corner of the living room. An unlikely crew. Strangely, it wasn't awkward at all. We had a lot to talk about. Gabe. The arrangements. The fact Gabe was a multimillionaire and nobody even knew it. My Uncle Jeff kept saying "millions?" I said "yes, millions ... maybe tens of millions. The attorney couldn't tell us exactly how much, of course." It was still hard for me to believe too.

Flora hopped up suddenly. We forgot all about the food. Everyone was hungry by this point. And it actually turned out to be the perfect amount. We even had a little left over. We were all stuffed, and Rebecca and I were emotionally and physically running on empty. Dad and Jeff had just driven eleven hours—part of it in ice and snow. *Thank goodness for Jeff's monster truck,* I laughed to myself. We were all just sitting there unmotivated to clean up—or even move—when there was another knock on the door.

I slowly got up. *Maybe we were making too much noise.* I thought ... *I don't normally have this many visitors at once. Maybe it's the landlord downstairs.* Instead, it was a lady in a blue plaid coat ... attractive ... maybe close to fifty. She was holding a beautiful white poinsettia. She said, "Laine? Are you Laine Anderson?" I hesitantly answered, "Yes." She said, "I'm Jen. You knew my mom." I'm scanning my brain. *Her mom?* I'm drawing a blank. Then she turned her head to the side as an ambulance passed by. Lily. She had Lily's exact profile. "Lily?" She nodded. "Yes, of course, I knew your mom."

As I motioned her to come in, she handed me the Poinsettia. As I was making a fuss over how it was the prettiest white poinsettia I had ever seen, Rebecca rushed over to help me find a good spot for it. Flora pointed out that there was just enough food left for one more plate. Jen accepted some dinner. I realized she was probably just being polite. But putting a plate together for her at least gave me something to do as we worked our way out of the awkwardness.

As Rebecca helped Jen with her coat, Jen said, "Laine, I'm so sorry about Gabe. I heard. I know you were dear friends. He is the one who told me you were helping my mom transition."

The word struck me ... "transition." I guess I had heard it put that way. But it hit me differently. I said, "I did. I guess."

"I wanted to thank you in person. Seriously, Laine. You have no idea what that meant to me that you took the time to be there with her. The nurses told me everything you did for her. It was so hard. She tried living with me. There was just too much history. And I was afraid that if I spent too much time with her, I would say something I would always regret."

Her eyes filled with tears. I took her hand. Then, I looked at her and said, "Seriously, it was a gift. I believe that sometimes things happen for a reason. Your mom helped me transition too. Thank you for trusting me with her."

She smiled. Neither of us seemed to feel any need for me to explain what I meant by my own "transition."

Everyone made their way to the kitchen. Dad and Jeff took a seat at the table with Jen while she finished her plate. The rest of us took care of the other dishes. James washed, Flora rinsed, Rebecca dried, and I put away. It had gotten dark. I stepped over to the living room and turned on a lamp. And as I did, James flipped on my fairy lights above my sink. Jen looked up at my sign and smiled.

Chapter 15

O Christmas Tree

Rebecca returned home but asked me to go to her church on Christmas Eve. I'm not going to lie. This made me nervous. It was like a recovering alcoholic going to a bar on New Year's Eve. I said I would think about it. But she went on about how they did this "Living Christmas Tree" where the choir members actually stood in the tree and sang. *What does that even look like?* My curiosity got the best of me. And she was persistent.

She picked me up around five o'clock. The program started at six. Her church felt a lot like the one I grew up in—except ten times bigger. It took up a city block. But there was the same feel. The same church smells of coffee and newspaper. The same hymnals. The men in suits at the door welcoming us in could have been any older man in my church growing up. There were three big screens instead of the one in my church. And The Living Christmas Tree was a sight to behold. It must have taken them all year to build it. As the choir members filed in, they dimmed the lights, and the tree lit up. I was genuinely excited. It was incredible.

There was about thirty minutes of Christmas music. I was surprised that some of the songs were even "secular." "Jingle Bells," "Rudolph." There were kids dressed as presents that twirled around the front of the tree. Santa made his way around the church, handing out candy canes. The singing and choreography were flawless. Rebecca looked over at me. She was proud. I was glad I came.

Just as I thought the program was over, the minister stepped up to the front from his pew. The lights went back up as the choir members filed from their places on the tree to doors behind it. The minister praised the performance. Everyone clapped. Then, in a serious tone, he said, "How many of you know for certain that you would go to heaven if you died going home tonight?" *Geez. Here we go. I know his song and dance ... word for word. And I know that he's holding back. He's a yeller. I can tell.* Then, he said, "We are going to show you what Jesus Christ has done for each one of you." The lights dimmed again.

First, there was this thundering noise, and red lights shone on the front of the sanctuary. There were these figures in black masks and capes running about, and a red Devil chasing them. That scene only lasted a few seconds. Then, some men quickly ushered a cross to the front of the church where there was a clanging noise. A narrator described Jesus' hands and feet being nailed to the cross. More thunder. Then a spotlight appeared on a man who portrayed Jesus with fake blood all over him and his white robe. The red lights turned off and on. Thunder boomed.

So, let me recap this. It was only about twenty minutes before that dancing children twirled around the front of the church to "Jingle Bells" while Santa passed out candy. They now sat at the front of the church watching a member of their church dripping in fake blood—on Christmas Eve. I felt sorry for these kids. And I felt manipulated. Tricked. It must have shown. I could feel Rebecca tensing up beside me.

Then, as quickly as all of that happened, the cross was whisked away, and the lights went back up. Now, the choir dressed in angel costumes filed in from the back of the church singing "Amazing Grace." Two teenagers rushed in a backdrop of painted clouds. The choir joyfully sang a few songs before the Jesus returned, all cleaned up in a white robe and long sandy-blond wig. He walked in and hugged each member of the choir. Everyone was suddenly laughing and overly jovial. The choir finished up their last song and the minister returned to the front. It was the altar call and then the collection. Several people went up, and we sat there quietly as the choir angels prayed over each one.

When we finally made it back to Rebecca's car, things were beyond awkward. Our egos weren't tangoing like before. It was more like just an abrupt disconnection. We had just sat and watched that performance but saw it much differently. I finally broke the silence. I searched for the good.

"That choir was amazing."

"Yeah ... they've been singing together for years."

I said, "You can tell. And those kids. Wow. Look out Broadway. That one little girl with the curly brown hair. She must have taken dance since she popped out of the womb."

"Aren't they adorable?" she said. Awkward silence. Then she blurted something out that floored me. Absolutely floored me. "Laine, do you think Gabe was saved?"

Suddenly, I realized where all of the sobbing came from. Rebecca was wondering all along if Gabe had just been thrown into the pits of hell. Gabe. Our Gabe, who lived like a pauper ... just donated millions to benefit dying patients ... kind ... caring ... loving Gabe ... burning in hell for eternity.

I took a deep breath. This was the test of all tests. I was still raw. I missed him so much. I said, "Why do you think he wasn't saved, Rebecca?"

"Well, he didn't go to church. I know that. I just never heard him say he was saved. I blame myself for never asking. I should have asked." She hung her head. She was truly remorseful. It was so twisted but so innocent at the same time.

I suddenly felt this deep love for her. An almost painful compassion. She was truly tormented by this. How could I be angry at her for it? I had a million things I could have said in that moment. But I didn't say one. I couldn't undo what religion had done to her. I couldn't "fix" her more than she could fix me. And neither of us had any hard and fast answers. *Nobody does.* I just said, "Rebecca, I guess we don't know who is saved or not. But if Gabe isn't in heaven, nobody is making it into heaven. Nobody. And to be honest, if the Gabes of the world aren't there, I don't want to be there either." Holding back tears, she shook her head. "I don't either."

We got back to my apartment. She reached into her back seat and grabbed a gift wrapped in silver Christmas paper. I said, "Ugghhh. Rebecca! We didn't say we were exchanging presents." I could tell by her face that she wanted me to open it right there. So, I carefully tore the paper away … trying to act excited. And after that conversation, it took all the acting I had in me. There it was—the most Rebecca thing I have ever seen in my life. A hot pink Bible with a floral pink and lime-green fringe. My monogram in lime green smack in the center.

She smiled. "Do you like it?"

I said, "I love it, Rebecca. I do. I love it."

"Well. I didn't think you had one."

I let her believe that I didn't. I held it to me. "Thank you. Thank you for everything, Rebecca. *Everything.* Really."

***

Ripples

I spent Christmas Day lounging around my apartment. There was more snow in the forecast. I had learned to enjoy being alone. And, of course, I got some goodies from the Nature's Market to celebrate. A basil and tomato quiche, a couple of pomegranates, some chocolate bark with all kinds of nuts and seeds, some fresh chicken salad from the deli and freshly baked sourdough bread. Some cranberry juice and ginger ale. I think I watched four Christmas movies back-to-back. I cried at each one, of course. It was cathartic. I had talked to my parents on Christmas Eve. But the girls wanted to call me again on Christmas Day and tell me everything that they had gotten that morning. They went through the long list. First ... Andrea. Then ... Audria. Then, they both were on the phone letting me talk to Gus. If he could have cursed me, I know he would have.

Audria said, "Oh, oh, oh. We didn't tell you about the man with no legs."

I said, "What in the world are you talking about? No legs?"

Andrea said, "The man we visited with no legs. He gave us candy. And the other people ... that one lady told us a story ... and I got to ride in a wheelchair ... and and and we took presents."

They went back to torturing Gus and trying to get him to "talk to me."

Mom finally got back on the phone.

"What in the world are they talking about 'man with no legs?'"

She said, "Oh, The VA Hospital." Your Uncle Jeff took the girls yesterday and delivered gifts and candy." She moved on like it was no big deal. I decided to act like it wasn't either. But maybe it was a big deal. Maybe it was huge. Maybe it was Gabe's ripple. Uncle Jeff had even been touched by it.

After we hung up, I lay there on my couch, smiling. I thought ... Gabe is still alive and well in this dark world. Alive and well.

Chapter 16

Soul Food

The service was beautiful. The hospice did two huge floral pieces at the front of the church. There were three eulogies. Mine was last. I made it brief but hopefully impactful. I read the Beatitudes. I touched on how Gabe exemplified them. And I tried to wrap up with some funny things about Gabe. That wasn't difficult. Gabe was funny. I told them about the time he pranked me into thinking my car was missing ... and the ongoing rearranging of each other's desks. They were silly and pointless pranks but made work more tolerable. Gabe made life more tolerable. James and Flora came to the service and sat with me. I felt a strange calm up there. A higher purpose and friendship can help us do impossible things, I guess.

There was tons of food. The line wound around outside of the fellowship hall. I was starving. James and Flora couldn't stay. I looked for Rebecca. I guessed she was probably talking to some of the hospice staff. I went ahead and got in line and pulled out my phone to text her. When I raised my head, I realized I was right behind Jacob Bell.

I said, "Oh ... hey ... wow ... that service was amazing."

"It really was. You did a great job on your eulogy."

"Thank you. That means a lot."

"And you just about made me cry."

I laughed. "Well ... my goal was to lighten things up. Gabe was funny, you know. I wanted everybody to remember that part of him."

Jacob said, "Oh ... I do know how funny Gabe was. You definitely succeeded. And it doesn't take much to make me cry. I'm a softy."

Then, his phone started buzzing.

"Dang. I've got to take this."

"It's okay. I'll make you a plate."

He yelled back, "I'll eat anything. Just nothing with mushrooms." He made a choking face.

I got both of our plates and looked for Rebecca and somewhere to sit. I thought, *Maybe she is in the kitchen bossing people around.* There were two seats at the very end of a table. I hurried to grab them. As I was getting ready to start eating, Jacob was back and dropped down into his seat with two desserts. One piece of lemon meringue pie and a giant piece of chocolate cake.

"This client is about to do me in."

I laughed and said, "By the way, how did Gabe find you?"

"Oh. My aunt used to represent Gabe's mom. She was her attorney. Our families have been friends for years. I think she's here somewhere."

He was looking around the room for her and said, "It's been a minute since I've been to a 'covered dish' but do you know what I want to know?"

I thought he was serious. "What?"

"Why is it called a covered dish? Can you bring uncovered dishes?"

I almost choked laughing.

He kept on and on ... "What if I just brought a plate of uncovered cookies? Uncovered potato salad? Uncovered fried chicken? Deviled eggs? What would they do to me? Would I be banned from covered dish dinners forever? Is there a covered dish jail, Laine?"

I was probably just delirious from the whole day, but I was laughing so hard I was snorting. This made him laugh. The people around us began to smile. It was contagious.

We finally pulled it together. And as I finished my plate, I noticed he had eaten everything I had chosen except one thing.

I said, "Oh noooo! Are there mushrooms in that dish ... or was it just not covered good enough for you?"

He threw his head back laughing again. Belly laughing. I never made anybody laugh like that. And I loved his laugh. It was deep and soulful. Then, he pushed his plate forward to show me. I looked more closely. He made that choking face.

I said, "potatoes *au gratin*?"

He said, "No offense. It's awful. Whatever it is … covered or not."

Then, he suddenly switched gears and said, "Oh. By the way … do you know anyone at school who might be a candidate for the scholarship?"

"I might. What are the requirements?"

"It's for med school. A student who plans to work in hospice care. It's a pretty big deal. Full ride."

I thought, *this can't be happening.* I casually said, "Let me think about that one" like my heart didn't just skip about four beats. Then, I pushed the lemon pie aside and said very Gabe-like, "Who puts lemons in desserts anyway? I really just want a bite of that chocolate cake."

Jacob pushed the plate with the chocolate cake squarely in front of me and looked me in the eye with a sudden seriousness that I don't think either of us understood. And said, "It's all yours, Laine. All yours."

And this is where my God story deepened … and widened to include so many soulmates. Rebecca, Jen … the patients and their families that I have now loved and served as their physician. James' and Flora's recent addition "Scout." And of course—Jacob—who I believe to possibly be the perfect mate to my soul. I still have miles and lessons to go, but I'm learning to trust life's timing. I still disagree with a lot that my pastor taught about the nature of God when I was a kid ... my first God story. But there was one thing that he said that stuck with me. He said life is a tapestry. And if you turn a tapestry over, it might look a mess. It might even appear chaotic. But there is perfect order, and every strand crossing another serves the grander plan. And God is woven through all of it. He was certainly right about that.

Behind You

There is a wanting of God
So much
That you are willing
To forsake everything
Godly to find him.
Ponder this,
The God who is beyond
What is godly.
Know this, that you may have to leave
More than you ever imagined
Behind.

Meister Eckhart

About the Author

Elizabeth Ferrell Casey is a high school teacher and former freelance health writer with a passion for inspiring thought in others. Her work has appeared in publications such as *Healing Lifestyles & Spas, The Well Being Journal,* and *Natural Health Magazine.*

Elizabeth lives with her husband and youngest daughter in a charming historic town in East Tennessee. She hopes her writing will help guide seekers and wonderers on their own magical, yet sometimes challenging, journeys.

Connect with her on Instagram:
@elizabeth_casey_author

9 781965 334263